RIPTIDE

The Secret Life of Trystan Scott
Vol. 3

YAParanormalRomance.com

This book is a work of fiction. Names, characters, places, and incidents are either the product of the author's imagination or are used fictitiously, and any resemblance to actual persons, living or dead, events, or locales is entirely coincidental.

Laree Bailey Press
First Edition: Nov 2012
ISBN# 978-1481209052

RIPTIDE

THE SECRET LIFE OF TRYSTAN SCOTT
VOL. 3

H.M. Ward

Laree Bailey Press

rip-tide: a strong current of swiftly moving water that flows away from the safety of the shore.

CHAPTER 1

~TRYSTAN~

Trystan's fingers skimmed Mari's cheek and then tangled in her soft curls. They stood at the foot of the stage, surrounded by empty seats. That kiss was still burned onto his lips. He couldn't step away from Mari. His eyes locked with hers, never blinking, never straying from her intense gaze. The moment felt so fragile that Trystan was afraid to breathe. Everything he ever wanted was standing in front of him, looking up in shock.

Mari's body shivered in his arms when he told her that she was the reason he wrote that song. Swallowing hard, Trystan breathed, "The girl who brought me to my knees, was you." Taking a breath to steady his voice, Trystan lowered his gaze and looked back up at her. "That song meant everything to me. It was as close as I thought I'd get to you. I've made too many mistakes, too many times. And then, like an idiot, I flaunted them in front of you." A smile lifted the corners of his lips as he allowed a curl to fall from his fingers. "Mari, I don't know what made you do it. I realize that you wanted someone for one night, but that isn't what I'm looking for anymore." His lips curved like he was trying to form a word that wouldn't come.

Mari shivered, unable to hold her body still. When she finally spoke, he could barely hear her, "You love me?"

It was a question that he wanted to answer every hour of every day, but when she asked, when her lips parted and those words tumbled out, Trystan felt a pang of panic pierce his middle. She wanted a plaything. S*he doesn't want you that way*, he thought. It felt like fingers were pressing into his throat and cutting off the air. The way

Mari looked at him—it was too much.

There was a slight tremor building in his hands. To hide it, Trystan slipped his fingers off her face and into his pockets. Looking at her through the pieces of dark hair that hung over Trystan's eyes, he said softly, "It's more than that. God, Mari." He sucked in air, and ran his fingers through his hair. "There's so much to say, and I have no idea how to say it. I wrote it down, because otherwise all those words, all those feelings, stayed trapped inside of me, in here," his fist banged on his chest as he lifted his gaze and met hers. Stepping toward Mari, he confessed, "I love you. Everything I am, everything I hope to be, is better when I'm with you. I don't know..." Trystan was breathing hard, like he'd been running from something terrifying.

Mari watched him, her beautiful brown eyes impossibly wide, with her lips parted in shock. As he stumbled over his words, lacking the normal Trystan Scott confidence, Mari stepped toward him and took his hand in hers. Brow pinching together, she looked up at him, asking, "Why are you trembling?"

Trystan worked his jaw, freeing the thought that was stuck in his throat, "Love destroys, I believe that—but I'm hopelessly in love with you." His head tilted to the side as he said it, his blue eyes so soft and vulnerable. "What am I—" he started to ask, but she cut him off.

Heart pounding wildly, he couldn't stand it. In that moment, Mari didn't say much. She just stood there shell shocked after he said he loved her, but Trystan had to tell her. She had to know. There was no way he could let her think, after all this time, that he was in love with someone else. But when he said he loved her, she didn't say it back. The center of his chest felt hollow, like a carved out pumpkin. He couldn't breathe. His mind was telling Trystan to make a joke and run—do what he always did—but he couldn't, not now, not with Mari.

The corner of Mari's mouth curved up. She held his hands tighter and pulled them to her chest, "Do you feel that? My heart's pounding in my chest like it's going to explode. You do that to me. You make me crazy. You make me better. You make everything better. You're the brightest part of my day and you always have been. I don't want a fling, Scott," he recoiled when she said his last name, but Mari pulled him closer, not releasing his hands, "I asked you that question last night, because I couldn't stand seeing you every day and sitting next to the guy that stole my heart, and act like everything's okay. When Tucker said you were enlisting—" she let out a rush of air, eyes wide, locked on his face, and continued, "I couldn't lose you. Not without even trying. How could you think I didn't love you?"

Trystan listened to her speak. His mind was trying to pull out of the conversation before his heart was blasted to bits and splattered across the auditorium walls. Mari could destroy him. One word and his life would never be the same, but as she spoke he couldn't help but smile.

When she asked that question, Trystan finally met her gaze. "You love me?" he asked.

Mari nodded, smiling up at him, "I love you, Trystan Scott, every bit of you; past, present, and future." A grin twisted her pink lips. Mari looked at him out of the corner of her eye, "Besides, it's not like I can turn it off. If that were possible, we wouldn't have had that kiss."

Trystan laughed softly. The sound filled his chest, making him feel whole. Leaning toward Mari, he used every drop of boyish charm he had, "I really liked that kiss."

Mari's cheeks flushed as she smiled, and she quickly tried to look at the floor, but Trystan didn't let her. Instead, he reached for her face and tilted her chin up. Smiling, he took in every inch of her red face and instantly wanted to cover her in kisses, "And I suppose you didn't like it as much?"

Mari smiled broader. “You’ll just have to do it again and find out… see for yourself.” She looked up at him through her lashes, her cheeks growing hotter in his hands.

“Is that so?” Trystan asked, a soft smile spreading across his lips.

She nodded, “Very much, I’m afraid.” Mari glanced up at Trystan. He pulled her closer and lowered his face, inching slowly toward hers. Mari’s head tilted to the side and he was kissing her again. Her arms wrapped around his chest and she held on tight. Trystan’s palms stroked her cheek as he pulled her lips to his. She tasted like strawberries and sunshine. He couldn’t get enough, he’d never get enough of Mari.

The bell rang and shocked them apart. Trystan stepped back, his gaze filled with mirth and his lips twisted into a perfectly boyish smile. He crossed his ankles, and bounced on the balls of his feet for a second, drinking her in like this was a dream. "I have more things I'd like to discuss with you, beautiful kiss ninja, but I have to get to class. I can't miss another or I won't graduate, because believe me—if that weren't the case—I'd stay here with you."

Mari looked at him, still beaming, "Go on, I understand." Trystan nodded at her, and grabbed his books. He was half way up the aisle when she blurted out, "Wait! Trystan,"

When he stopped and turned back, he saw concern on her face. "What's the matter? Awh, screw it. I can stay." He threw his books on a chair and walked back down the aisle. Mari met him halfway and laughed.

Grabbing his books, Mari shoved them into his hands, and said, "No, you can't. Besides, I just wanted to ask you if we can keep this a secret, for now. I'm not really supposed to date. If my Dad finds out, well, I just don't want to deal with it…"

Trystan fought back the urge to reach out and run his fingers through her soft curls again—to be that close to Mari, and to be able to touch her…

Trystan felt like he could fly. There was nothing that could bring him down. Leaning toward her, he touched his forehead to hers lightly, "My lips are sealed. I won't tell a soul." He smiled at her again, beaming with excitement. Pulling away from her was torture. He shouldn't have gotten so close again. Tearing himself away from Mari was the last thing he wanted to do, but Trystan couldn't miss another class.

As it was, he was on thin ice. Tucker saved his ass earlier and he knew it. Who would have thought that today would go this way? Trystan didn't. Grinning at her, he sucked in a deep breath, letting it fill his chest before turning away.

"Better get going," he said, his voice a little too high, almost like he was laughing. When did it become so hard to hide how he felt around Mari?

CHAPTER 2

~MARI~

"Yeah, you better go." My voice was soft. It was everything I could do to keep it from shaking. *Trystan Scott loves me.* He said it. He wrote a freaking song about it. A song that went viral. A song everyone knew. My heart lurched in my chest as he pulled away from me and turned to walk up the aisle.

He looked over his shoulder at me, those brilliant blue eyes gleaming.

"The view's good coming and going, I hear."

At that point, the smile on my face increased to mega-wattage. I glanced down at the floor and back up at him, feeling the blush spreading across my face. Looking up at him from under my lashes, I nodded once and said, "Only you would say that."

"Only you would pretend you weren't looking." Trystan walked backwards up the aisle, one sneaker squeaking as he clutched his books tightly to his chest. The way he looked at me made everything else melt away. I didn't remember where I was or what I had to do next. The only thing that mattered in that moment was Trystan. He was like a beautiful black hole, and he absorbed every piece of me.

I teased, "I'll make a note to ogle you more openly next time."

He held out his arms, his books extended away from his body and balanced on the top of his palm. "Why wait?" Trystan was standing right in front of the door. I could hear kids moving through the halls, heading to their next class. Trystan turned in a circle slowly, keeping his gaze on me the whole time.

I laughed. Closing my eyes slowly, I opened my mouth, not knowing what to say. I wanted to look at him. I wanted him to see me do it. I don't know why, but the moment felt charged. Every spot on my skin was hypersensitive, and when his eyes passed over me, I flushed harder. I've never blushed so much in my life.

Breathing raggedly, I folded my arms over my chest to try and hide it. "Very pretty," came out when I finally spoke.

Trystan's arms fell to his sides, and his books slapped against his leg. He ran back down the aisle to me asking, "Pretty? Seriously?" His brows disappeared under his hairline, as his soft lips hung opened waiting for me to respond.

I grabbed his shoulders and twisted him around, pushing back up the aisle, shoving him toward the door. "You're such a drama queen.

Get to class already!" Trystan allowed me to push him up the aisle. I could see the laugher in his eyes as he looked over his shoulder at me. When we were standing before the door, he dug in his heels and turned suddenly, which resulted in me smacking into his chest. It would have been sexy if I didn't have that just-walked-into-a-pole expression on my face.

Trystan wrapped his arms around me for half a second, and whispered in my ear, "There are so many words to describe you. I plan on telling you all of them later." He pulled back and kissed my temple before releasing me. His eyes met mine and held. "I can't believe it."

"Neither can I," I replied softly. We stood a step apart, not touching, just gazing at each other. The bell rang again, but he didn't move. "You're late."

"So are you," there was no more laughter in his voice. Those radiant eyes bore into me, cutting past every defense mechanism I had. That gaze stripped me, causing me to feel everything at once, making me realize exactly how much Trystan affected me. My heart pounded harder in my chest, as a shiver worked its way down my spine.

After a second, I knew why he didn't want to leave. This felt surreal, like everything would vanish like smoke in the wind when he left. I didn't want to say it, but it was the only way to vanish the fear. "Everything will still be the same after class. Go. I don't want you to get in trouble because of me."

Reluctantly, Trystan turned and put his hand on the door. He looked back at me, like he was going to say something else, but he turned and pushed through the door instead. I watched the door slowly close, until I couldn't see Trystan anymore.

When he was gone, I sucked in a sharp breath of air. It felt like I didn't breathe the entire time he was here. The tension flowed out of my body, and I threw myself into the nearest chair. The theater was dark, save for the safety lights spilling off the stage.

I sat there, alone, in the darkness wondering what just happened. Staring at the empty stage, I felt like my life just took a turn. It was one of those moments that mattered, where I could feel it and I knew this incident was important. This wasn't a fling. No, it was more than that. Trystan loved me. Somehow, we finally came together.

Maybe living like a lunatic wasn't a bad idea. I would have never done anything like that a year ago. Crossing a room and throwing my lips on a guy seemed like something someone else would do, but I did it—and it worked out. It made my life better, it dramatically changed everything.

I stared at the spot where we stood, where Trystan told me that I was the girl in the Day Jones song. My gaze fell to the floor. A scrap of white poked out from under the chair. Rising slowly, I walked toward that piece of paper like it was my destiny. Those words were Trystan's heart poured onto paper. There was no mask, nothing hiding any part of him. That was what drew me to the song in the first place.

Reaching down, I picked up the paper and held it in my hands. The entire song covered the front and back of the page. Trystan's familiar handwriting lined the margins, along with codas and breath marks mingled amongst the lyrics.

Grasping the page in my hands, I looked down at the last line. Mari. My name was there, written in thick dark lines. Pressing my eyes closed, I shuddered and pressed the page to my heart. I was the girl who brought Trystan Scott to his knees. I was the girl he fell in love with.

CHAPTER 3

~TRYSTAN~

The rest of the day passed sluggishly. The clock seemed to tic slower, like it was stuck in tar. Trystan leaned back in his seat after taking a verbal beating for being late, like it mattered. He was out of there in a few months. These last few weeks were fluff, filled with busy work. Trystan hated busy work. It was a waste of time. He'd rather have a test than do another bunch of worksheets and endless essays.

Trystan's mind drifted back to Mari, the way her lips felt against his. Trystan got that far off look in his eye and totally missed that someone was talking to him.

"Mr. Scott, will you please share with the class your thoughts on the matter." The teacher was already beyond irritated with him today.

Trystan straightened in his seat like he was going to answer, but after a moment, he smiled sheepishly and shrugged. "I'm sorry Ms. D'Miagmo, but I don't know." There were a few sniggers from the girls behind him, but Trystan ignored them. He also ignored Brie. Her gaze was burning a hole into the side of his face.

"Mr. Scott, please take this class seriously or I will ask you to leave. You must have an opinion on the matter, and since opinions aren't right or wrong, I want to hear yours." She arched a gray eyebrow at him and folded her arms over her chest. The woman could have been a schoolmarm. She just needed a wooden ruler and permission to beat kids over the head with it.

Trystan smiled at her, but knew it was pointless to try and get any sympathy. D'Miagmo had it in for him. There were some teachers that decided on day one that they didn't like him. He had no idea why, but there was always one teacher who thought he had an easy life and needed to be taught a lesson. Ms. D'Miagmo was that teacher.

Trystan opened his mouth, but Brie cut him off, "Ms. D'Miagmo, I think it's obvious that Trystan feels uncomfortable answering this question because of his religion. Isn't it against school policy to discuss faith issues in the classroom anyway?" She flipped her golden hair over her shoulder and blinked her big blue eyes at the teacher.

Ms. D'Miagmo sucked in air through her nose like a horse. Now Brie was in the line of fire. "Brie dear, and what religion does Trystan practice that he can't discuss this matter?"

Brie looked up from her nail like she was thinking about getting a manicure. "He's a conservative Baptist," she said with utter certainty, and then added, "and everyone else here is Catholic or Jewish so it's not right to press him on this. Faith issues aren't open for debate in public school."

The teacher arched an eyebrow at Trystan. "So let me get this straight? You can't discuss women's rights because it makes you uncomfortable… because of your religion?"

Trystan smiled once like he was uncomfortable and nodded, "Yes, I don't want a pack of rabid women to attack me in the hallway because you forced my conservative beliefs out of me."

D'Miagmo looked like she might cry… or scream. She looked down her nose at Trystan, not breathing or blinking. Trystan couldn't tell if she was having an aneurism, and had never been so glad to hear the bell ring. Trystan knew not to stay another second. Scooping up his books, he bolted for the door, but Brie was right behind him. Trystan pushed his way into the crowded halls.

"Don't I get a thank you?" Brie said, chasing him down the hall.

Trystan wove through the crowd, stopping at his locker. He didn't look at Brie. Gripping the lock, Trystan spun the dial, and opened the metal door. "What for? You made me look like a sexist jerk. Some crazy chick is going peg me with a stiletto in the parking lot later, you know." He tossed in his books and slammed the door shut.

Brie grabbed Trystan's arm, and twisted him toward her. "Nah, a woman likes to be owned sometimes. If you were handing out..." her voice trailed off.

At that moment, Seth rounded the corner. Trystan's shoulders tensed at the sight of him. Brie stopped talking and turned around to see what made Trystan respond that way. "What the hell was that?" Her gaze followed Seth, noticing an equally tense look from Trystan's best friend.

"Nothing," Trystan said after Seth passed. They both glared at each other like old enemies. It made Trystan's guts twist. Why couldn't Seth be happy for him? Why'd he have to hate Mari so much?

Brie muttered, "Could have fooled me." When Trystan didn't respond, Brie stepped in front of him. "Well, I just wanted to say that rehearsal yesterday was fun. I'm looking forward to it later." She wrapped her lips around each word, saying them with such a sexy voice that Trystan forgot to glare after Seth.

Instead his head snapped back toward Brie, eyes wide. "What?" he tried to step away from her, but Brie had other plans.

She lifted her hands and draped them over his shoulders, playing with the hair at the base of his neck. "I know that kiss yesterday was real, and it's okay. I'm willing to pretend that we're not into each other, but I know the truth."

Trystan shook her off. "What are you talking about? That was acting and nothing more."

Brie's ruby lips pulled into a smile that said she disagreed. "I know what's real and what isn't, and I'm saying it's okay. We don't have to let anyone know." She winked at him before turning on her heel, "It'll be our little secret. See you later."

With that she was sauntering away from him, her hips swaying as she walked. The bell rang and several guys just stood there, staring at Brie's ass as she walked down the hall. Trystan stepped back and leaned against the row of lockers, slamming his head against them. She thought it was real; she thought that kiss was hers. Crap. Brie had the potential to make nothing look like a whole lot of something. Trystan took a deep breath and decided to deal with the fallout when it came. There was no point in trying to figure out what move Brie was going to make next. He'd have to wait and deal with it then.

CHAPTER 4

~MARI~

Trystan lay in my arms on the old couch. It was the last period of the day. We both managed to sneak away and meet in the basement before practice. The stage above was empty. I touched Trystan's hair lightly, pulling my fingers back, over and over again. His hair felt like silk.

"That's nice," he said sounding a little sedate. Trystan seemed like he was running on fumes lately, like he hadn't slept well in weeks.

I smiled softly at him, touching my hand to his cheek. "Can I ask you something?"

He looked up at me, and a playful smile twisted his lips. "What could you possibly want to know? I've told you about every stupid thing I've ever done." He laughed, "And for some reason, you love me anyway."

Hearing the word was new. Mari wanted to say *love* as freely, but it stuck in her throat. *Give it time*, she reminded herself. *This is all new*. "Yes, I do. And I always will. I'm good like that." My fingers stilled as I looked straight ahead.

Trystan felt the tension and took my hand in his. Stroking my palm with his thumb he said, “Ask me anything. I’m yours Mari.”

Heart beating rapidly, I looked down at him. It wasn’t something that I wanted to ask him, but it had to be done. “Trystan, I’m so glad today went the way it did. I mean, I couldn’t have dreamed something like this would ever happen, but I’m not sure my friends or family will understand—or approve. It’s not you, it’s me, and it’s selfish. I can’t tell them about us. Not yet.” My tongue felt like cotton as it crashed into my teeth, making my words sound harsher than I’d intended.

Trystan lifted his hand and ran his fingers gently along my cheek, making my stomach flip. “Anything you want. If you don't want to tell anyone, don't. I told you already and I meant it. We can keep this a secret, Mari. That's fine with me."

"You're not mad?"

Trystan laughed. Looking into her eyes, he said, "Mad? How could I possibly be mad? My dream girl is holding me in her lap, she steals kisses, and she's so beautiful that I can barely breathe when I'm around her. This is a dream for me, Mari. I'll do anything to be around you, to let me love you." As he spoke, his fingers tangled in my hair and he pulled me down for a brief kiss.

Everything about him made me feel like I could fly. My stomach lifted inside of me as my heart raced faster.

His kiss was so soft and so hot at the same time. He pulled away before I was done, leaving me wanting more.

Trystan looked up at me. “It’s a secret until you say otherwise. Okay?”

I nodded about to say something else when the door above us scraped open. Trystan jumped up and shot across the room. Trystan slumped back in the tattered old chair he frequented and dangled a leg over the arm like he’d been there all along. The click of female shoes descended the stairs and I knew it was her before Brie rounded the corner.

“Hey losers,” she said, grinning at Trystan. Brie glanced at me once, her gaze sliding over my outfit like she thought I was a fashion nightmare. "Cutting? Really Trystan, and this close to graduation?" She folded her slender arms across her ample chest, "And you kept the *thing* with you."

Have I mentioned that I hated Brie? Bristling, I retorted, "Nice to see you too, granny panties."

Trystan snorted a surprised laugh. Brie glared like she wanted to kill me with her eyeballs. If she was a robot, Chinese stars would have flown out of her pupils and sliced my head off. "Don't you have somewhere to be, you little leech? Nobody wants you here. They just pity you, and humor Tucker, so they can graduate." She glanced at Trystan, but his expression remained impassive. I wondered if he wanted to punch Brie in the face. The thought made my fist clench. I didn't notice until my nails bit into my palm.

Trystan glanced at me for a second. His eyes were light, but the set of his lips let me know he was seething underneath. I shook my head carefully, so Brie wouldn't see. If he defended me now, everyone would know about us. I had to keep a secret. If my parents found out, I was toast. They'd lock me in my room for eternity.

Trystan's brow lifted ever so slightly as he regarded Brie. "If you're planning on starting a cat fight, let me run and get a few of the guys." He grinned wickedly at her and leaned forward like he was serious.

Brie's face contorted and she laughed one short burst, "As if I'd waste my time pounding Mary. Get real."

Before I could say anything else, Trystan cut me off, "Then why are you down here?"

Her ruby lips pulled up into a seductive smile, "I already told you. The bell's about to ring and I thought that we could practice the second act, alone, before everyone got here." Her voice dripped with sexuality, as she walked toward him.

I'm sure flames erupted from my ears, but my lips were locked. My fists balled harder, my nails cutting through my palm.

Trystan grinned at her, and tilted his head to the side as if he were admiring her. That was going to take getting used to. If no one knew we were dating, every single girl in the school would still be throwing themselves at him. If they knew he was dating someone, the normal girls would back off.

Brie wasn't normal. She was a no-holds barred kind of girl and wanted what she wanted. What I didn't understand was why she was hitting on Trystan like this. I mean, she has a boyfriend.

When Trystan answered, his voice was playful. "Thanks, but I already practiced it with Mari." He jumped out of his seat and stretched his hands over his head, which caused his dark tee shirt to hike up and reveal his flat stomach. It felt like I fell down a mine shaft, my heart jumped up into my throat as I hyperventilated. I stared. I couldn't help it. Trystan was hot and he was mine. As the thought drifted across my mind, a smile drifted across my face.

Trystan said, "Meet you upstairs," and walked away from Brie. He winked at me as he passed, his sapphire eyes glittering.

Brie stood there with her hands on her hips, watching him take the stairs two at a time. When she turned back to me, her smile turned rancid. "You need to stay the hell away from him, bitch. Do you understand me?"

The butterflies that were fluttering in my stomach moments ago were blasted away by Brie's words. While Brie was rank, she'd never confronted me like that before. I tried to act like she didn't bother me. Still slouching back into the couch with my feet kicked up onto the coffee table, I asked, "Or what? Or Tucker won't pass Trystan. I bet he'd be real grateful if you arranged that for him."

Brie stood in front of the table with her hands on her hips before her boot crashed into the cheap wood. It jarred my legs from the table top, jolting me upright on the couch. "You listen to me and listen good. You've been getting in my way, and don't think I haven't noticed, because I have. Whatever you think you have going on," she waved her finger in a circle, indicating all of me, "isn't working out for me. So stop, or you'll find yourself somewhere you don't want to be." Her eyebrows lifted as she cocked her head, making her earrings sway along with her golden hair.

Sitting on the edge of the couch, I gaped at her. Was she serious? Brie ruined people, but it was through rumors and carefully making their lives miserable. What could she do to me? At the same time, this didn't sound like that kind of threat. I wanted to stand up and punch her in the face. Everything she did, everything from the way she acted like she owned the school to the way she assumed she could claim Trystan whenever she wanted, pissed me off. Something inside my brain snapped. That fist that I'd been holding launched from my lap and pulled me to my feet, as it made a beeline for Brie's perfect nose. When my fist and her nose collided there was a crunch followed by a deafening shriek.

Brie's hands flew to her face as she screamed, "You heinous bitch!" Before Brie could do anything else, she turned and fled, running up the metal stairs as fast as her high-heeled shoes would carry her.

I stared at my fist in horror and pressed my eyes closed. I sat back down on the couch and leaned forward, burying my face in my hands. What have I done? As if I wasn't in for it before, Brie will kill me now. I'd be a smudge on the sidewalk by this time tomorrow. I punched her. I cracked her nose.

Noise filled the stairwell overhead and multiple pairs of shoes descended in rapid thumps like they were running. Katie's voice rang out, "I leave you alone for two periods and you punch Brie in the face?"

"I'm sorry?" I said, almost apologetically, looking up surprised to see her. "What are you doing here?"

Katie laughed, "What am I doing here? Saving your ass. Brie was ranting at the top her lungs to Tucker. I was passing by and heard her say your name, so I stuck my head in. He's coming. Sound sorry. And next time you break Brie's nose, I better be there to see. We could have had this up on YouTube. With that shriek, it would have gone viral."

"Oh God, don't say that." Panic was setting in. It wasn't until then that I noticed the owner of the second set of feet.

Mr. Tucker stood behind Katie with his arms folded across his chest.

Neither of us realized he was standing there. Katie turned slowly, like the girl about to get killed in a horror movie.

Tucker breathed, "Get out." Katie nodded like a dashboard dog and ran up the stairs without looking back. Before I could explain, Tucker said, "You too, get out. I don't want to see you on set again."

"Mr. Tucker, let me explain."

"Explain what? That we're days away from a show and you broke my lead's nose. And for what? Because she was mean to you? Ah, I've got some news for you, Mari—get over it! You take everything to heart. You always have. Brie's Brie. She's got thorns around other girls, I know. I see it, but you don't see anyone else punching her in the face, do you?" He sighed deeply, his face returning to a normal color and shook his head. "What's with you kids today? It must be a full moon. Scott attacks his best friend and now you. You, out of all people, picked today to throw a punch." He breathed deeply as he looked down, his fingers pinching his nose.

"Mr. Tucker..."

"I don't want to hear it. Just go, Mari."

It never fails. When something totally awesome happens, something equally bad blindsides me.

CHAPTER 5

~TRYSTAN~

Practice was weird. Trystan stood on the stage as the completed set was being erected around him. The stage crew raised the flats one by one, installed doors, and touched up some of the paint. Now it looked like a real room, filled with furniture and picture frames. As the stage crew did their thing, the guy in the lighting cage was muttering to himself. His voice carried to where Trystan stood a few feet away. The house lights were flashing on and off instead of dimming. The lighting cage was nearly fifty years old and due for an upgrade, but with the school budget the way it was, they'd never get one. Whenever a budget vote came up, people showed up in drones to vote it down. It didn't matter what was on the ballot. The roof could be caving in and the town would still vote against it.

Trystan kept thinking about Mari. A smile leaked across his face. He couldn't help it. That kiss. And the way she felt laying in his arms. For a small moment, his life felt perfect. Happiness was always something just out of reach for Trystan. Whenever it came along, it was swiftly yanked away. This time, Trystan would make sure he didn't mess up. Mari mattered too much to him. Everything about her made him better, made him think he had a chance. Trystan wouldn't be another statistic.

Waiting in front of the lighting cage, Trystan stood with his hands in his pockets wondering where Brie went. When Brie finally surfaced from the basement, she ran straight into the girl's bathroom at the back of the stage. Trystan turned to watch Brie flee with her hand over her nose. His heart sank when Tucker followed a few moments later, pointing one of his chubby fingers at the stage door. Katie and Mari left without looking back. *Shit. What'd Brie do now?*

Practice took too long. It was close to opening night. Brie acted hysterical. Tucker forced Brie on stage with her nose bandaged and an ice pack taped to her face, which severely screwed with her head. Brie couldn't get a line out without stumbling or messing up. Tucker didn't bother to try the second act. They skipped over that part like it didn't exist, which was fine by Trystan.

After practice, Trystan grabbed his books from his locker and looked around for Mari, but the school was deserted. He walked past the diner on the way home, hoping to find her inside, but she wasn't there. Sighing, Trystan pushed his dark hair out of his eyes. The wind blew harshly, flipping his hair over his head and into his eyes again. Trystan tightened his jacket, wishing he had something warmer to wear. The leather was nearly worn away in places, giving the frigid air a way to leak in.

It'd been a long day and it felt good to finally be out of the school. Trystan just wished he'd seen Mari before the end of the night. Curiosity was part of it, and Trystan wondered how Mari waked away without a scratch and Brie had a bloody nose. Hurrying, Trystan pushed on toward his house, crossing the train tracks, and walking quickly to his front door.

When Trystan walked into his house, he came face to face with his father. The old man's eyes were bloodshot. There was a piece of paper in his left hand. Dad was left handed, just like Trystan. *God, they were too much alike*, Trystan thought as he walked through the threshold and closed the door behind him. He ignored his father's eyes on his back as he went to the kitchen looking for something that would pass for dinner. Trystan was always hungry lately and there was never enough to eat. Placing his books on the table seemed to be what set his dad off. Suddenly he was yelling like Trystan did something horrible.

Dad stood behind him, his voice was sharp enough to cut glass. "You think you're too good for us. That's what's wrong with you, you know. Always walking around like you own the place." Dad slurred his words slightly, telling Trystan that tonight was going to suck.

Standing with the fridge door open, Trystan froze. It took a moment to recognize that the scrap of paper in his father's fingers was a picture. When Trystan did, his heart dropped into his shoes. Trystan grabbed whatever food was left, which wasn't much. He took a few slices of bread and the peanut butter he'd gotten from Sam's deli and made a sandwich as fast as he could.

His father droned on and no matter how hard Trystan tried, he couldn't drown out the words.

"You're the reason she left. This," he said, pointing to everything, "is your fault. Me and my whole fucking life got reduced to this because of you, and you stand there like you're so damn proud."

Trystan couldn't help it. He knew that he shouldn't speak, but he did. His jaw was tense, the words fell out of his mouth before he could stop. "Maybe she left because of me, but you did this to yourself. Things didn't have to go this way, Dad. You did this. Not me."

Before Trystan could blink his father was across the room and screaming in his face. "You think I didn't try! You think I fucking chose this?" Dad bellowed and spit went flying, sticking to Trystan's cheek. His father laughed with such rage that Trystan stepped away. When Dad spoke again, his voice was low and menacing, "That's right, boy. Blame me. You did *nothing*." The old man's rank breath lingered in Trystan's nostrils, but his dad finally stepped away.

Trystan went to pass by his father, but was clotheslined. His father raised his arm at the last second, trapping Trystan, before grabbing Trystan's hair with his other hand, and yanking his son back to his chest. The picture of Trystan's mother was clutched under his father's thumb. Thrusting it in Trystan's face, Dad made him look.

When Trystan tried to wiggle free or look away, his father only tightened his grip and forced him harder. "Look! Look at her! Look at those eyes, and how they seem so steadfast, like they'd never leave. You destroyed everything!" He shoved Trystan toward the hall that lead back to Trystan's room. "Get out of my face. I can't stand to look at you!"

Trystan's chest felt like it was ripped open with a rusty nail. Every muscle in his body was tense, ready to fight, trying so hard to hold back. Trystan's jaw locked tight to keep from speaking, but the one thing he wanted to avoid the most was that picture and he'd already seen it. Stumbling back to his room, Trystan pushed through the door. His mind screamed, protesting that he should fight back, but something held his rage in check. Taking purposeful breaths, Trystan walked down the short hall, trying to steel himself, trying to make his heart go numb before it shattered into a million pieces.

When Trystan swung his door open, he meant to lock it and throw himself on his bed, but there was no lock, no bed. The walls were barren. The nightstand was gone. His closet door was open and the only thing inside were shadows. Trystan stood there, his hands shaking slightly, as he realized that his father threw out all of his stuff. Trystan felt his dad behind him but he didn't turn around. Rage flooded Trystan's body, making him want to act out, but he refused.

A hand shoved hard between Trystan's shoulder blades. Trystan didn't expect it and fell into the room. "Maybe this will teach you that you're no better than the rest of us." Before Trystan could turn around his father yanked the door shut. It wasn't until then that Trystan realized that the doorknob was turned around. The sound of metal sliding against metal alerted him to the lock closing.

"No!" Trystan screamed and threw himself at the door, but it was too late. His fists beat the door, but it was solid, the kind of door that was used at the entry of a house. Trystan knew, because he put it there when he traded it out for the thin particleboard version that had originally been there, in order to keep his father out.

"You never learned your place, Trystan. I swear to God, I'm going to teach it to you." The hallway fell silent.

Trystan felt the panic slide up his throat. The room was dark. The lights were gone and the fixture that hung from the ceiling had no bulb. Racing to the window, Trystan pushed it open, but the bars kept him from getting out. The cold air rushed in over his face. Trystan turned around and leaned his back against the wall, clutching his face in his hands. He slid down until his back was under the window, hoping that his father would see reason in the light of day, but there was no way to know. Dad had done stuff like this before, when Trystan was little and couldn't fight back. He'd lock Trystan away for hours, sometimes days. When it seemed like Trystan would die of thirst, the man finally showed his face and let him out. Trystan tried to be good after that, but it didn't seem to matter what he did or didn't do—he was never good enough.

Tucker's words rang through Trystan's ears like a gong, ebbing and pulsing. *Someone told you wrong. You're worth something.*

Lowering his head to his knees, Trystan fixated on the words, but they couldn't penetrate his heart. Tucker's words couldn't strip away years of being told he was the reason for his father's grief. Trystan's chest felt hollow and he let the numbness overtake him.

CHAPTER 6

~MARI~

"Have you lost your mind?" Daddy screamed. He'd been pacing in my room since he got that phone call from Brie's father.

There was nothing I could say that would calm him down, but that didn't mean I wouldn't try. "What was I supposed to do? She threatened me!" Tears streaked my face. I couldn't help it. I cried when I was angry.

Daddy turned on me, roaring, "*What were you supposed to do?* Get the teacher! Not punch the girl in the face. Her father is threatening to press charges. Do you know what that means? Do you have any idea? We could lose everything because of you!"

Sucking a ragged breath, I screamed, "There was no teacher, there was no help! Maybe I shouldn't have hit her, but why can't you even act like you care about me? You didn't even ask me what she did! You just assumed that everything was my fault!" I trembled with my hands balled into fists at my sides.

If there was ever a wrong thing to say, that was it. Daddy blew up.

His eyes widened, before he started screaming in a blind rage. The verbal assault went on, but I couldn't process what he was saying, not when he looked so livid. I backed away from him, but he kept coming at me like he'd hit me. My heart pounded in my chest like I was running away from an axe murderer.

Things weren't supposed to be like this. Daddy was supposed to defend me. He was supposed to protect me, but instead, he looked like he was going to kill me. After what seemed like forever, my Mom came in. It seemed to calm Daddy down enough to realize that his hands were shaking, lifting toward me like he was going to do something.

Dropping his hands, Daddy shook his head fiercely and walked away from me. He shoved past my mother and left the room, leaving a wake of anguish behind.

All the fright that had built up in my body exited my mouth in loud sob that sounded more like a scream. My mother stood there, staring at me with disgust. "You brought this on yourself, Mari. Clean up and go to bed." She turned away and left without another word.

After they left, I heard them arguing in the kitchen. The conversation was about lawyers and settlements. They seem to think that Brie's father had his sights set on their money. I wanted to scream and jump up and down in front of them. Since when does money matter more than people? I didn't realize I was so disposable. My entire life, I thought they'd stand up for me, but they didn't. The only thing they cared about was protecting their money and their precious careers.

I plucked my phone from my backpack, knowing it was insane to try and use it, but I wanted to talk to Trystan. I needed him. He'd understand, but I didn't have any way to contact him. I sat on my bed sniffling as I stared at the phone. I didn't want to talk to Katie. She'd tell me to suck it up, that this was part of having the perfect family—so what if they flipped out once every sixteen years? She didn't understand. Her family fought all the time, but this wasn't a fight. This was something else. It showed me where my place was in this family, and I didn't like it.

The next morning my eyes were puffy. When I sat at the table my mother said nothing, handing me my breakfast like everything was normal. "Your father and I are on for the next four days. I made your dinners for each night. Come straight home after practice and eat. I'll check on you when I get home." She poured a glass of orange juice, smiling like a saint.

I nodded, not wanting to talk about it. It was fine by me if they worked seven days a week. I did my best to eat my breakfast, but I wasn't hungry. I just wanted to get out of there and go to school. When I cleared my half-eaten plate, my mother said, "You don't have to be so dramatic, Mari. I know you're upset, but you still have to eat."

I just looked at her. I couldn't think of what to say to make her fathom how betrayed I felt. She dropped me off at school without another word. As soon as she pulled away, I felt better. Four days on my own would help. They'd come home from work in time to drop me off at school. We'd barely see each other.

After going to my locker, I looked around for Trystan. He usually haunted this hallway before first period, but I didn't see him. I went to class, listening to the teacher droning on. I didn't get a chance to look for Trystan again until our free period. When I walked into the auditorium I heard Tucker speaking softly and rapidly to Trystan, "…is not okay. You can't skip class like this and then expect to walk at graduation in June. If there's something you need to tell me, some reason for your tardiness, tell me. You don't have to fight the whole damn world by yourself."

"I'm fine," Trystan used a tone that said he was finished talking about it. When Trystan turned around, I saw an angry red gash marring his cheek.

The smile I had on my face faltered and slipped away. Tucker looked at me and then back at

Trystan. When I was closer, Tucker said, "Talk some sense into him," as he jabbed his thumb at Trystan.

"What are you talking about?" I asked, not understanding.

Tucker sighed, "Ask him how he got that cut on his face and make sure he had a tetanus shot. He won't talk to me."

Trystan's shoulders tensed as he looked after Tucker, who was walking away, "That's because there's nothing to tell." Tucker walked through the door and left us standing in the aisle alone. The empty seats surrounded us on all sides, the stage lights dim and glowing golden. When Trystan looked back at me, his expression softened, but the slant of his mouth said he still thought he needed to defend himself, and I didn't want that.

Before he could speak, I said, "I only want to ask you one thing."

"Really?" the corners of his mouth tightened again. "And what's that?"

"Will you hold me?" Tears welled up in my eyes and streaked down my cheeks. Trystan instantly became the man I knew, and forgot about his worries. Stepping forward, I walked into his arms, and he held me tight.

CHAPTER 7

~TRYSTAN~

When sunlight poured into Trystan's room earlier that morning, he tried the door. Still locked. Glancing out the window, Trystan saw that his dad's car was gone. *Shit.* Trystan stretched, his back aching from sleeping on the hard floor. His dick of a dad turned the heat off so that he was freezing, too. Although it was cold, Trystan refused to close the window last night. It was better than being trapped in the darkness. It was a good thing Trystan didn't take off his jacket when he walked through the door.

Running his hands through his hair, Trystan looked at the door. He knelt in front of it wondering what time it was, if he was late for school yet. The teacher's would ride his ass, threatening to not let him graduate. Some tried to threaten him by saying he couldn't walk at graduation—like that was a threat. He didn't care if he walked or not. It's not like anyone would show up and clap for him. No one cared what happened to Trystan Scott. While the other kids got pats on the back and ushered off to college, Trystan got a psychotic parent who blamed him for everything.

Trystan stared at the lock, wishing he could remember his mother—at least a little bit—but there was nothing. No voice, no sense of safety, no warm memories of his mother cradling him in her arms or kissing him good-night. It wasn't something that he usually dwelt on. That was the past. There was nothing Trystan could do to change it. She left. No amount of wondering would bring her back, and Trystan had no plans of looking for her either. What was the point of chasing someone who left him behind? Trystan had had enough misery from the time she left. The thought of finding her and having his mom turn her back on him again was just too much. It wasn't worth the risk. Not now, not ever.

Staring at the golden lock, Trystan realized his Dad changed the knob. Trystan could have picked the lock if it was the old one, but not this thing. Rising, Trystan stood back. He took a deep breath, braced himself, and kicked his boot into the door. The door shook, but it didn't give. Trystan kicked it again and again, trying to weaken the frame, so that it would crack and let him out, but the jam was too strong. Again, another of Trystan's ways to protect himself came back and bit him on the ass. After a few moments, he was huffing and the door gave no indication of opening. Trystan sat down on the floor hard, and banged his head back into the wall.

"I have to get out here," he muttered to himself.

He stared at the black bars that shuttered him in. They were solid. There was no way he could bend them or slip out between, they were too narrow. Pushing himself to his feet, Trystan walked across the room to the window. If he drew attention to himself, someone might call the cops, and Trystan learned early on that cops were bad. If they showed up, he'd be in a worse situation than he was already in.

Trystan leaned on the windowsill and turned his head, making his cheek press into the cold bars. They were jagged with rust. The paint on the bars had blistered and peeled long ago. When Trystan pulled his face away, he felt the grime on his cheek and wiped it away. It left an orange smear on his fingers. *Wonderful.*

Trystan stared at the bars, wondering if he could manage to kick them. They were a little loose, like the mortar holding the bolts in place had grown weak. Trystan's hands clenched at his sides. Before he spent more time thinking about whether or not he'd get into trouble, Trystan kicked. His boot came up and punched the side of the frame hard. To his surprise, his foot kept going. The bars went flying to the ground and bits of brick flew back into Trystan's face. One piece of shrapnel collided with his cheek, raking a deep cut as it flew by. Trystan swore, but he didn't have time to look at the cut. The window was the only way out. He was wearing the same clothes as yesterday, didn't get to shower, and now his face was covered in rust and blood.

Trystan swung his leg over the windowsill and jumped out. He landed next to a dead bush on the other side of the wall, and ran to grab the bars. Lifting them, Trystan wedged the rusty metal back in place. To his surprise, it held. The only problem now was making sure the school didn't throw him out when he got there and then he'd have to deal with his dad later.

When Trystan walked into the high school, Tucker was in the lobby. Trystan stopped mid-step and swung around, ready to bolt, but Tucker grabbed him by the shoulder.

"You missed first period, Scott. What do you—" Tucker stopped speaking as Trystan whirled around. His chubby jaw slipped opened for a second, before taking a deep breath. "What happened to your face? Is that rust?" Tucker lifted his hand like he was going to touch Trystan, but stopped when Trystan flinched.

Trystan didn't mean to wince, but so much had happened. He was overly tired and his body was reacting without thought. *Shit. Shit. Shit.* Trystan tried to laugh it off, by saying, "If you're suggesting that I—"

But Tucker cut him off, "Save it, Scott. Nurse's office. Now." The smirk fell off Trystan's face. They walked down the hall in silence. Why did things have to be like this? Why was Tucker gunning for him? Trystan grew more defensive, which made his wit so sharp it stung. When he walked into the nurse's office, Tucker followed.

"I don't need a babysitter," Trystan said in a snarky tone, but Tucker ignored him.

"Glenda," Tucker said as he crossed the room to the nurse's desk. "This one looks like he was hit in the face with a rusty bucket, but he won't say what happened. Can you take a look at it and clean him up?"

"Sure," Glenda said, eyeing Trystan. She'd always been kind to Trystan, but he didn't want people fussing over him. It just made things worse. She told Trystan to sit in the chair next to her desk. When he didn't move, Tucker gave his shoulder a shove.

"How'd this happen?" Glenda's voice was kind. She bent over and examined the cut, careful not to touch him.

Trystan's insides were twisting. Fear clung to his throat in thick clumps, making it difficult to swallow. *They're going to find out. They have to know*. Trying to muster his charm, Trystan said, "I ran into a burning building and saved a few babies on the way to school. I must have stepped on a rake on the way in."

Glenda grinned at him, "Always a kidder," she leaned closer, her fingers pressing on Trystan's cheek. He forced himself to sit still even though it was sore. "So this is rust?" Trystan nodded. Glenda stepped away and got a brown bottle and some cotton balls.

She dabbed the cotton with the stuff in the bottle and then on his cheek. "It might sting a little," she said too late. Trystan didn't flinch this time. He sat rigid in the chair, staring straight ahead. As she patched

Trystan up, she spoke about the weather and other things that nobody cares about.

At some point Tucker left, because he was alone with Glenda. That was when she said, "Did someone do this to you? It looks like you were hit in the face with a shovel."

"I wasn't," Trystan responded, his voice flat.

"Maybe it was a brick, then? Or something else that bruised your face? Trystan, when was the last time you had a tetanus shot?" It didn't matter what she said after that. He didn't answer. Glenda was young enough to still be patient. When Trystan wouldn't answer, Glenda touched her hand to her forehead and said, "I'll have to call your father and ask."

Trystan wanted to jump out of the chair and run from the room. Suddenly he was more cooperative. "I don't need one. I'm fine. And thanks for cleaning me up. You were always my favorite nurse."

Her hands were on her hips as she watched Trystan inch toward the door with a smile on his face. "Wait, I haven't bandaged that yet. When you smile, it's going to bleed."

"It's okay," he said over his shoulder, exiting the room. "I'm fine. I'll come back if it opens up again."

Trystan's heart was pounding. His nerves were like brittle old wires, ready to snap. When he turned down the hallway, Tucker was standing against the wall, his massive arms folded across his chest. There was no way to get away from the teacher. Tucker insisted on talking. They'd gone into the auditorium and Trystan found out that talking meant having Tucker question him for nearly the whole period and Trystan sitting there fuming, not saying much.

By the time Mari walked in, Trystan felt his sanity slipping away. Then, Tucker left and Mari had questions in her eyes. Trystan couldn't unwind. Watching his reflection in her eyes, Trystan saw a man that looked too much like his father. Trystan was ready to turn and leave her there if she pressed him for answers, but she didn't. Instead, she asked him to hold her and tears streaked down her cheeks. All the anger and fatigue melted away as Mari pressed her wet face against Trystan's chest.

His arms closed around her shoulders, holding her tight, wanting to fix whatever made her like this. Trystan ran his fingers through her soft curls, pushing it away from her tears, "What's wrong?"

Mari's body shook gently. When she looked up at him, he wanted to make her smile so badly. Tears didn't belong on that perfect face. Trystan's thumb wiped a tear away as it spilled from her eye and ran down her face.

"I'm sorry. I just had a really bad night."

Trystan pulled her close and held on tight. "I know what you mean. Mine was less than stellar, too."

"I would have called you, but I didn't know what your number was. Either way, my parents probably would have gone postal on me if they knew I was talking to you." She sniffled, trying to smile. Trystan felt Mari's back rise and fall as she sucked in huge, ragged breaths.

After a moment, Trystan suggested, "Let's go downstairs for a little while. I'll hold you all you want and we don't have to worry about anyone walking in and seeing us together. Sound good?"

The pulled apart and Mari looked up at him, nodding. When they got to the basement, Trystan flipped on the lights and they descended the stairs. No one was down there. No one was ever down in the basement during the school day.

Trystan sat on the couch and pulled Mari onto his lap. She fit perfectly, like she was made for him. When Mari leaned back into his shoulder, Trystan felt whole. The emotions that flooded him earlier were gone and he found himself wanting to confide in her.

Trystan squeezed his arms, which were wrapped around Mari's waist. She slipped her arms around him and held on harder with her face buried in his chest. Trystan could smell her hair. The mingled fruit scents filled his nose.

When Mari pulled back, Trystan asked, "Do you want to talk about it?"

She shook her head. "Not really. I finally stopped crying and there's only twenty minutes or so until the period is over. I'd rather just sit here like this. You make me feel so much better, I can't even tell you."

Trystan kissed her temple softly, pulling away slowly, like it pained him. "You make me feel better, too."

She smiled. It wasn't full wattage, but it was a start. After a second Mari said, "I've been banished from the theatre after school."

He nodded, “I heard. You punched Brie in the face.” He couldn’t help it, a smile spread across his lips as he watched her.

“I didn’t mean to. It just happened. One minute she was threatening me and the next my fist was crushing her nose.” Mari spoke quickly, like she couldn’t believe she was telling him this. Panic laced her voice, but he didn’t know why. It was a hit, and from what he knew of Brie, she deserved it. “Anyway, Tucker banished me for the rest of the semester, so I won’t be able to see you until after.”

Smiling, Trystan asked, “You want to see me after?”

Nodding, she said, "Yes. I was thinking about things—about what I posted on your Day Jones wall—and I've decided something." Mari spoke slowly, her eyes drifted to the floor as she spoke.

Trystan's stomach felt like it was in a free fall. Was she saying what he thought she was saying? He tried to stay cool and act like he didn't know what she was talking about. "What'd you decide?"

Mari was silent for a moment as she looked at the floor, with those long dark lashes blinking slowly. When she looked up at him, Trystan knew he'd give her anything she wanted. Her brown gaze was intent, focused on his face, making Trystan's heart race faster. Suddenly, he was much more aware of her weight on his lap, the curve of her hips in his hands, and the way her chest swelled when she breathed.

Staring at her lips, he waited for her to say it.

"I want to be with you."

Trystan's mind erupted with conflicting thoughts, both warring to win. But the thing that came out of his mouth was Mari's thoughts on the matter, not his, "But, you said you wanted to wait until you were married. I love you, Mari, but don't change things for me. That's part of who you are."

She looked into his eyes, pinning Trystan in place, making him want to squirm. "I need you," she said so softly that he barely heard it. When he didn't answer, Mari rested her head on his shoulder and said, "Please, Trystan."

The *please* and the way she said his name made Trystan come undone. Before he could do something stupid, he kissed her cheek and slipped Mari off his lap. The look of horror on her face struck him like a bat.

Quickly, Trystan said, "I can't say no to you. I'll do anything you want, be anything you need. I promise, but I'm not doing it in the school basement. You deserve more than that and if you keep sitting on my lap and talking about having sex with me, we won't be talking about it anymore." Mari's face flushed and she looked away. Trystan put his fingers under her chin and pulled her gaze back toward him. "I love that about you. I love how you can blush like that. Actually, I uh… wrote a song about it." Before he knew what happened, Trystan grabbed the guitar and was tuning it, talking about one of the songs he wrote for her.

"You wrote a song about me blushing?" Mari asked, surprised.

Trystan looked up from below his brow and smiled at her. "Sort of. It's about all the little things you do; the things that make me love you."

Placing his fingers on the strings to form the cord, Trystan began to strum. It was a song that was Mari to the core. It revealed more of Trystan's heart, but he didn't care. He wanted her to smile and he knew this would help. Trystan sang, watching Mari, as he slipped his hand across the neck of the instrument, allowing the notes to fill the air. As he played, her lips lifted into a smile and her brown eyes glittered just for him. Trystan couldn't help but smile back at her.

Everything about Mari was magic. She touched him like nothing else could, and honestly, the thought of having sex with her was equally appealing and terrifying. If a look from Mari could produce that much emotion, Trystan wondered what sex would do. If Mari had her way,

Trystan was going to find out. The song ended and Trystan remained where he was, across from her on a stool.

Mari stood with a sweet smile on her face and walked slowly toward him, her hips swaying gently as she came closer. "That was so incredible. The way you see things is so pure, so intense, and so vulnerable at the same time." Stopping in front of him, Mari took the guitar from his hands, making Trystan's pulse pound harder in his ears.

He watched her, saying nothing as she set the guitar down and stood in front of him. A smile spread across Mari's lips. "You think blushing is sexy?" She placed both hands on his thighs, splaying her fingers, leaning in close to his lips.

"I think everything you do is sexy."

"Kiss me," she commanded, and he did.

Trystan's hands threaded in her hair and pulled her mouth down on his, tasting her sweet, hot kiss on his lips. Heart hammering in his chest, Trystan let the kiss grow stronger and hotter, tasting Mari when she opened her mouth, and stroking her tongue with his. They were both breathing hard when the bell rang and shattered the moment.

Mari stood and stepped away, her hands shaking slightly. Grinning at him, she said, "You follow directions really good."

Trystan laughed. He stood and rushed toward her, snatching her up by her waist and spinning her around until she shrieked. When he set her down, Mari looked up at him smiling like everything was all right. After a second, Mari reached into her pocket and fished out a piece of paper and handed it to him.

"It's my address and my cell. Come by later, okay?" Suddenly, she was shy again.

Trystan looked at the address, and confusion pinched his face. "I thought you didn't want your parents to know?"

"They won't. They're working for the next four nights."

Trystan felt his heart speed up. The way she looked at him said she had plans for all four nights.

CHAPTER 8

~MARI~

After school, Katie sat with me at the diner. We ate a bunch of fried food and topped it off with ice cream. I was so nervous. I'm not sure what person took over my brain and invited Trystan Scott into my bed, but she was gone now and I was left with moody Mari who fretted over everything.

"What's with you?" Katie asked, dipping a fry in ice cream before popping it in her mouth. "You've been out of sorts for days."

I shrugged, "PMS?"

She laughed, "Yeah, right. More like boy-on-the-brain. Don't tell me that you're still pining over Trystan."

I shook my head confidently. That wasn't a lie. I wasn't pining over him at all. "No, of course not."

"Then what is it?"

I debated telling her what had me on edge. The question was could I tell her and omit names? I didn't know. And if Katie snooped, she'd see it was Trystan coming to my house later. I decided to risk it. I needed someone to talk to about it and I sure wasn't asking my mom. "You know how I was going to wait to be with someone? Well, I changed my mind."

Katie's jaw dropped open and the ice cream slipped out. It splattered on the table in one big goopy slop. Neither of us said anything for a moment. As she wiped up the ice cream glob, she asked, "What? Why?"

I shrugged, "I don't know. I thought it'd be romantic to wait for the guy who'd marry me, but now that just seems corny." Corny was the wrong word. The real reason was that I felt so alone and I thought that sex would make it better. I wanted to feel wanted.

Katie stared at me like I'd grown two heads. "Something's not right here, but I have no clue what it is.

Who are you and what have you done with Mari?"

"Stop it, Katie. I wanted to talk to you about it." My voice was serious, pleading almost. I felt stupid for bringing it up.

Katie noticed and became serious. In a hushed voice she said, "Don't do it. Having sex will bind you to that guy for the rest of your life. Be picky about who you're with. Honestly, I used to laugh at you, but when I see *him*," she couldn't stand to say her first boyfriend's name, "now, well, I think you had it right. I wish that I'd waited for someone that I wanted to be attached to forever."

Katie's eyes darted away from mine as she spoke, as if she were ashamed of what she did. "But it felt right at the time, didn't it? How were you supposed to know he wasn't forever?"

Katie laughed bitterly, "I knew, Mari. He wasn't the one. I just didn't bother waiting. Maybe it was stupid, but I didn't think I'd get another chance. Now I've learned that there's always another chance, another guy willing to do it. They're not picky when it comes to sex, so I figure I have to be."

"You think I'll regret it?" I asked, my voice nearly a whisper.

She nodded. "You sound disappointed. What did you think I would say? You see the way I avoid my ex. Whatever amount of fun I had wasn't worth worrying about getting knocked-up or contracting something gross. It probably sounds funny, but you rubbed off on me. I'm waiting from now on. The guy has to prove he loves me and stick around for a while before he gets into my pants." Just then the waiter walked by and nearly tripped as he overheard Katie. She was blunt and gorgeous. Hearing her talk about sex made guys salivate.

My gaze fell to the table as I played with my napkin.

Katie asked, "Are you going to tell me who he is?"

"Not yet."

CHAPTER 9

~TRYSTAN~

Trystan looked at the piece of paper in his hands. Theatre practice had dragged on, mainly because Brie refused to cooperate with her face looking the way it did, but it was finally over and he was on his way to see Mari. The streetlights cast a yellow glow on the pavement. The night air wasn't as frigid as last evening.

Trystan walked past Mari's house, not stopping in front. His heart raced faster, as his mind repeated the words she'd said earlier. Lowering his gaze, Trystan shoved his hands in his pockets and walked on. Circling the block, Trystan came up behind Mari's house, cutting through the neighbor's backyard to remain out of sight.

Although Mari didn't ask him to sneak up to her house, Trystan was too smart to be seen. No one wanted him around their daughter and Mari's parents were probably worse. She was smart, like really smart. They probably wanted to send her off to some Ivy League school next year and he'd never see her again.

Trystan sighed, pushing through the spot where the fences met. Neighbors might have looked cordial in this neighborhood, but they were cheap. That last inch of vinyl fence was an expense that no one wanted to pay, since it was covered by tall shrubs and trees. Trystan twisted sideways and sucked in to press himself between the gaps in the fence. No one saw him do it.

Within seconds, he was standing on Mari's back porch, looking up at the two story house, with his eyes fixated on the only bedroom with a light shining through the windows. Mari crossed the room, her hands stretched above her head, as she pulled her hair into a ponytail.

As if she sensed him, Mari stopped and turned toward the window. Slowly, she stepped to the sill and looked down. A smile slipped across her face. The window was already open and her curtains fluttered in the breeze.

Smiling down at him, she said, "You could have come to the front door." Mari had on a white cami and jeans. There was a patch of lace at the top of the cami, but the shirt was cut lower than anything she usually wore. It was the kind of tank top that Mari would have layered, but tonight she hadn't. Her arms were bare, her hair pulled up, and that smile on her face made Trystan want to climb up the side of the house to her.

"I didn't want to risk being seen. You know, by nosy neighbors and all that." Trystan had his hands in his pockets. He might have looked suave on the outside, but his pulse was pounding in his ears and the paper with Mari's address on it was getting strangled in his pocket.

Mari leaned on the windowsill. Her breasts curved beautifully, swelling, as she leaned on her elbows. "Are you sure this didn't have anything to do with, I don't know, being you?"

Trystan grinned. "What does that mean? Being me is pretty good, but you'll have to be more specific."

She laughed. It was that magical sound he loved. It reached deep into Trystan and he didn't want it to end. "The Romeo and Juliet thing, this little seduction scene you've got going on here. It's insanely romantic. If you showed up with your guitar and sang from below my window, I would have died."

Trystan snapped his fingers. His palms were so damp from nerves that they nearly slipped past each other without making a sound. "Damn it. I knew I forgot something."

Mari smiled down at him before straightening up. "I'll be down in a second. There's a door by the kitchen," she pointed the direction he needed to go, "I'll come down and open it up."

"But I was going to scale the wall."

"Don't you dare!" she said, still laughing and disappeared from the window.

Trystan walked in the direction she pointed and came to a leaded glass door made from thick wood. His heart dropped into his shoes. Not only was she smarter than him, but she was way richer. He was poor. Suddenly a rush of cold ran through his stomach and he wanted to leave. This was a mistake. There was no way they'd have enough in common, coming from such different backgrounds, but before Trystan could give it another thought, Mari threw open the door. She looked fantastic, her body all smooth curves and that bared neck was perfect for kissing. Trystan felt every inch of his body respond to her. If only his body listened to his brain.

"I'm glad you came," she said shyly, tucking a stray curl behind her ear. "I started to think you weren't going to show up."

Trystan walked past her and into the kitchen, trying not to gape. The kitchen looked like something that belonged in a showroom somewhere. His fingers found his pockets again and hid out in there to conceal the nervous twitch of his hands. "Practice ran late." Turning toward Mari, he said, "I wouldn't have missed this."

"Good." She held out her hand and Trystan reached for it, hoping she wouldn't mind how warm it was. "I mean, I'm glad you came. Not seeing you after school was weird. We're always together. Did you notice that before?"

His eyes slipped over Mari's body and her face flamed red. "Of course I noticed. I notice every inch of you, every day." He tugged her hand, pulling her into his arms. This was where she belonged. He could feel it. Smiling that wicked smile of his, Trystan said, "For the longest time, I thought you knew, and that you were just playing me."

"Ha!" she blurted out, and wrapped her hands around Trystan's waist. "I was playing you? You made me so crazy that I couldn't think straight. I had no clue you thought of me that way at all, I mean, why would you?"

"Are you kidding?" Trystan asked, his hands tangling in her hair, as he tilted her face up to meet his gaze. "You have no idea what you do to me, how you make my heart hammer in my chest, until it feels like I can't breathe another breath, how one look from those dark eyes sets my skin burning, longing for your touch, or how your smile sets me on edge and fills my dreams until I see you again. I thought you were doing it on purpose, but then I realized that you didn't know—that you were just being you and I was the one with the problem."

"The problem?"

"Yeah. I was hopelessly in love with you." He ran his fingers through her hair as he spoke, brushing the back of his hand against her cheek. She looked up at him with such wide dark eyes, eyes that didn't trust what they saw. She was afraid he'd hurt her, and Trystan felt exactly the same way.

After a moment, Mari looked down, breaking the intensity of the moment. "Come this way. I want to show you something." Trystan followed her through the dark house, their fingers laced together. As they climbed the stairs, he knew where they were going, to her bedroom.

Stopping in front of the door, she turned to him. "I thought we could hang out and talk for a while, if that's all right?"

"That sounds perfect."

Mari pushed the door open and a smile leaked across Trystan's face. She stepped into the room and turned to watch his reaction. He glanced around at the white moldings and thick trim around the door and window. There was a flat screen TV on one wall along with a stereo and iPod dock. A Kindle sat on her night stand, with a computer screen glowing softly on the desk next to her bed. The bed made Trystan pause. It was larger than his—well, the one his dad threw away—and was covered in a white and purple bedspread that had a cascade of ruffles on the skirt.

Trystan turned back to her, an eyebrow rising on his face in surprise, "Ruffles? Really?"

She shrugged, "What's wrong with ruffles?"

"Nothing," he said grinning, "it's just more girlie than I would have thought you'd have. I thought you'd be practical, a solid colored comforter kind of girl."

"I got it when I was twelve. Everything was purple, white, and unicorns. The bedspread was too expensive to toss, so the ruffle monster remains." Mari folded her arms over her chest as she spoke, like she was embarrassed a little bit.

"It's sweet. I can't picture you at twelve, wearing ruffles."

"I never wore ruffles. My mom wouldn't let me. She said ruffles made me look fat." She shrugged like it didn't matter, but Trystan could tell it was more than that. There was a rift between Mari and her mom. He'd heard it before, the way her voice sounded weary, like she'd given up on her mom.

Trystan didn't comment. Instead he crossed the room to a board decorated with ribbons. In the center of the board was a piece of paper with familiar handwriting. Trystan pressed his finger on the page and turned to look back at her, "Day Jones fan?"

"You know it. He's dreamy."

Trystan grinned and looked down for a second before meeting her gaze, "I thought I lost this. Some much happened that I didn't know where it went." It was the song he'd writen for Mari.

"I picked it up. If you want it back—" she reached past him to unpin it from the board, but Trystan took her hands and stopped her.

"No, it's yours. It's your song. I want you to keep it."

Mari looked at his hands and Trystan released her wrists. Mari walked across the room and sat on the bed, patting the spot next to her. Trystan felt like his body had frozen and turned to ice. For some reason, he couldn't move. It felt like he'd shatter into a million pieces. It wasn't like he hadn't done this before, but Mari made it different. Everything was intensified to the point he could barely breathe.

Sensing his apprehension, Mari said, "Come sit with me. We can watch TV or talk." She meant, *we don't have to have sex.*

The pit of Trystan's stomach was in a free-fall. He breathed in deeply and ran his fingers through his hair. "I'm sorry. I've known you forever, but this is…" he paused reaching for the right word, willing her to understand him, "this is too important. I don't want to mess it up."

Mari smiled at him and shook her head. Pushing off the bed, she crossed the room and grabbed Trystan by the wrist, "Trystan Scott, I swear. If you act like this when I say I want to watch TV, what will you act like when I say I want to sleep with you? Come here and sit. You won't screw this up." She yanked his arm, pulling him to the spot in front of her bed. He watched her, thinking too many thoughts to speak, but Mari just smiled at him. Wrapping her arms around his waist, Mari suddenly sat down and pulled Trystan down with her. They fell to the floor with a thud.

Mari laughed when she hit the floor. Sensing Trystan's tension, she said, "Hey, I'm still me. This is still us. Nothing's changed."

Trystan's smile faded as he sat up. Looking at her eyes, he whispered, "Everything has changed, for the better. Every time something finally goes right, something comes along and destroys it."

Mari leaned in and kissed his cheek, "You'll always have me, Trystan. No matter what happens, I promise my friendship is forever. Don't worry so much. Let's just spend time together the way we used to, but maybe you could kiss me once in a while, instead of torturing me with those sexy lips." A wicked grin spread across her pink lips.

The taste of strawberry lip gloss filled his mouth. Trystan was worried, but that was only because he cared about her so much. "Anything you want, kiss ninja. But, you gotta realize that I'm in uncharted waters here. I don't want to fall off the edge of the map."

Mari laughed, "What, are you a pirate now?"

"I know how much you like those puffy shirts, so yes. My eye patch arrives tomorrow. I ordered it directly from Davy Jones, so it's totally authentic. It'll be kind of soggy, but his customer service wench assured me that it'll dry out and have a nice sea brine coating."

Before he could finish talking, Mari's fingers found his waist and she started tickling him. Trystan managed to finish saying the snarky sea brine thing before retaliating. God, everything about Mari made him want to be with her. He was just so afraid of screwing it up.

No matter how much Trystan tried to worry, he couldn't with Mari's fingers wiggling against him. Every thought in his brain flew away as a massive tickle war ensued. Mari rolled across the floor, her smile and laughter intoxicating him further. She jumped to her feet a few times and Trystan jumped at her, knocking her back down and slipping his hands under the hem of her shirt. Her soft skin felt perfect. When Mari looked like she was about to cry, he'd let her wiggle away, only to repeat the scenario again.

Holding Mari close and hearing her laughter made him so high. If Trystan could stay like that, with her forever, he would.

CHAPTER 10

~MARI~

The look in Trystan's eyes faded, as my fingers found flesh under his shirt and tickled. Trystan squirmed and wiggled, periodically laughing harder than I'd ever heard him laugh. The tickle fight went on until I'd rolled across the room twice. I had no idea how much time passed—a few minutes maybe—but when I looked at the clock it was past eleven. How'd it get so late?

Trystan reached for me, his fingers snatching at my waist and he pulled me closer. Positioning himself above me, Trystan held me in place, tickling me until tears leaked from the corners of my eyes, and I was screaming like a lunatic.

That's when I cheated. I totally lost. He had me pinned, but I couldn't stop looking at his lips. Trystan's mouth was so close and that smile was so sexy. I wanted to taste it. Trystan's grin dissolved when my lips pressed against his.

Without a word, the tickle fight was over and he was on top of me. Trystan's hands found my face and stroked my hair while his kisses grew hotter. Teasing me at first, Trystan's teeth gently nipped my lower lip like he was hesitant to do more. He lingered there, pressing small kisses to my mouth and gently nibbling my lip, teasing me until I couldn't stand it.

Heart racing, I slipped my hands under the bottom of his shirt and found his back. Trystan's skin was hot and smooth. Lifting my fingers, I held him closer, pulling him tighter against my chest. We were both breathing hard, like we'd been running for miles. I was so hot, so lost. I needed him so much. Trystan had no idea, but I decided I wouldn't mention sex again, not after the way he acted before. I expected Trystan to be happy about it, but instead he seemed skittish.

I lay in his arms and enjoyed Trystan's hot kisses and the sensation of his full lips pressing against mine. Heat seared through me, swirling in my stomach until my nails bit into his back. I didn't mean to. It just happened. That's when he finally kissed me. I mean, kissed me fully, deeply—the way he felt he should. The kisses up until that point were like he was holding back. Passion surged through us and things got hotter. If I could have pulled Trystan closer, I would have. I couldn't get enough of him. Everything from his scent, to the way his skin felt beneath my fingers, to the way his muscles rippled beneath my touch made me want him more.

I was kissing Trystan Scott. No, it was more than that. He loved me and he was showing me what that meant, how he wanted to tease me with kisses until I lost my mind.

"Trystan," I breathed his name. He broke the kiss and looked down at me breathing hard. We were both covered in a thin sheen of sweat. "I love you."

Dazzling me with a pure smile, he said, "I love you, too."

We stayed like that for a moment, both of us breathing hard, just staring at each other. The way Trystan's gaze moved between my eyes and my lips made me want to kiss him more. When his scorching look drifted lower, I knew I was toast.

We had to do something else or I wouldn't be able to stop.

As if he was reading my mind, Trystan sat up causing a blast of cold air to rush between us. "I'm thinking that I don't have the self-control I thought I did." Trystan gazed at the window with a sheepish look on his face. It was so sweet.

Laughing softly, I pushed myself up on my elbows and looked up at him. "Neither do I." Scooting over behind him, I threw my arms around his shoulders and squeezed hard, hugging him from behind. Trystan nearly fell over, but I held him against me. After a second I released him, and Trystan turned around to look at me. I knew what he was thinking, that he should leave. It was insanely late. My parents would have killed me if I stayed out this late.

Before he could say anything, I asked, "Stay? Just a little longer? You have no idea how much better tonight is compared to last night." The smile slipped off my lips. I couldn't keep the bitterness out of my voice.

Trystan sat on the floor, his arm draped over his knee, with those sapphire eyes softly searching mine. Finally, he nodded, "I can stay a while longer. I just want to be gone by the time your parents get home. I don't want to get you in trouble."

"They're working the seven to seven shift and they usually get breakfast before coming home, so unless you stay all night, there's no way you guys will run into each other." I looked at him for a moment, wondering why he wasn't antsy about missing his curfew, so I asked, "What time do you have to be home?"

Trystan smiled. It was the one that said he was going to evade the truth, but not quite lie. "There is no time. I don't have a curfew."

Sitting across from him, I felt my head cock to the side like a confused Pomeranian. "Seriously?"

He shrugged. "Seriously." It felt like he was leaving something out, but he didn't say what and I didn't want to push him.

"Then, stay here as late as you want. Oh, and since you don't have a cell phone, I want you to have this." I crossed the room and opened my closet door. Fishing out a box from the top shelf, I turned around and handed it to him.

Trystan had crossed the room and was standing behind me. He looked at the box and bristled a little. "You're giving me a phone? Mari, I can't take this." He tried to push it back into my hands, but I shook my head.

"Yes, you can. It's one of those cheap throw away phones. I bought it a few months ago because I lost the super-expensive phone my dad had gotten me. I bought that one and forwarded my calls to it until I found this phone." I pointed to my smart phone on my dresser. "I can't use this one and no one has the number. I thought it'd work good for us, you know, so I can hear your voice at night—so you can get hold of me, if you need to." I felt fragile for some reason. I didn't want him to say no, but I could see it on his face. He didn't want it. After a second I said, "I'm sorry. I didn't mean to make you—" Pressing my eyes closed, I shook my head and snatched the box back from his hands. I turned to shove it into the closet, but Trystan's hands fell lightly on my shoulders.

His voice was level, but when he spoke there was an intensity there that I'd never heard before, "What happened last night? Did someone hurt you?"

I turned toward him. Tears stung my eyes but they didn't fall. I shook my head. His eyes searched mine like they were trying to find the truth. I wanted to tell him, but I couldn't say it out loud. *My parents don't care about me. I'm alone.* My throat tightened and I couldn't speak, even if I wanted to.

Trystan looked down at the box and took it out of my hands. "I'll borrow it for a while. I want you to call me if something like that happens again."

I couldn't help it. The tears flowed over my eyes and ran down my cheeks. I wrapped my arms around his neck and Trystan held me.

I had no idea how much time passed, but when he stepped away I felt like everything might be okay, and it wasn't because he took the phone. That was symbolic. For some reason Trystan didn't want it, but he took it anyway to make me feel better. He put me first. No one did that for me before. I smiled and cried like a crazy person until Trystan's shoulder was soaked with tears.

Trystan kissed my temple softly and said, "Tell me what happened when you're ready. I'll always be here for you, Mari. And if anyone ever hurts you—" he left the threat hanging in the air. I nodded and pulled away.

I sat down on my bed and before I knew it, I was recanting what happened last night. Trystan stood for a while and then he finally sat next to me. By the time I finished, he had his arms around me. "It's stupid," I sniffled. "I'm crying because I got yelled at. I sound like a brat."

"No, you don't." He kissed my wet cheek and held my face between his palms. "And that's not why you're crying. I know you, Mari. I know what this is about." He stroked my hair away from my face, and then I leaned into his shoulder, staring blankly ahead, not speaking. It was silent for a moment, until he whispered, "We're more alike than I thought."

Lifting my head, I asked, "What do you mean?"

Trystan didn't meet my gaze. Instead he looked down and stared the floor. "Our fathers—they seem to have unrealistic expectations. That's all. It's kind of paralyzing." I nodded, wondering what his father did to him. Trystan seemed so hard, so cynical at times. He constantly had a wall up that blocked everyone out, but somehow I snuck through. "I was going to leave after graduation, but things kind of changed."

My heart beat faster as hope flooded through my veins. "You're not going to enlist?"

"And leave you?" he grinned. "Nah, I'll have to move onto plan B, which has something to do with staying here with you."

I threw my arms around him. Trystan embraced me and we stayed like that. I couldn't help the smile on my face. When he pulled back, I said excitedly, "You should go down the Day Jones path and see where it leads." Trystan didn't look convinced. "Your songs are powerful, they speak to people, and I've seen you on stage—you glow. People can't help but love you. You'd be really good at it."

Trystan's gaze cut to hers. His mood was a tad off, apprehensive maybe. "You really think you'd want to share me with all those people?"

"I want you to be happy."

"I'm happy here with you. You're all I need." Trystan's thumb rubbed the back of my hand. His eyes drifted to my lips and I knew he wanted to kiss me again. Trystan broke the gaze, like he was trying to control himself, and looked at the clock. "It's nearly 2:00am. You're going to be a zombie tomorrow. You should get to sleep."

I nodded. Lethargy had been pulling on my body like giant sandbags. "So should you."

He looked down, and ran his fingers through his hair. "Yeah. I will."

Liar. What's with him tonight? I thought about it for a moment, what it could mean, and stumbled on the answer. "You don't sleep, do you?"

Trystan's blue eyes lifted to mine, nervous like I'd wound him. "It's okay. Listen, you can stay here until dawn, if your dad won't mind. If you don't want to sleep, you can watch TV downstairs, eat something—" He was staring at me with his lips parted slightly. I couldn't read his expression. Trystan seemed to be caught between terror and surprise and I had no idea why. "What?"

Trystan smiled sadly and shook his head. That haunted look slipped away like it was never there. "Nothing. You're just amazing. I'd like to stay longer, if that's okay with you."

"Of course it is. Let me get ready for bed. I'll be right back." I dressed for bed, pulling on a pair of sleep shorts and a cami. I crawled into bed, and pulled up the blankets. Trystan sat at the foot of the bed and smiled at me.

"Will you stay until I fall asleep?" I blinked slowly, barely able to keep my eyes open.

"Sure, that'd be nice. And then I'll sneak out so your parents don't skin me. I'll see you at school in the morning." He stood and sat down again, closer to me, leaning in to kiss my forehead. My eyes fluttered like they wanted to close. I didn't want the night to end. It was so perfect.

Trystan started to sing softly, as he stroked my cheek. The result was instant bliss. The sound of his voice washed over me, comforting me. There were few things in life that were certain, but I knew this was real. We were meant to be together. My breathing slowed as I snuggled into my blankets. Trystan's gentle touch and voice lulled me into a sleep coma. I didn't wake up until my alarm went off the next morning. The night passed, and when I looked, Trystan was gone. It was like a dream, a wonderful dream.

CHAPTER 11

~TRYSTAN~

Trystan pulled his jacket tighter and looked back at Mari's window one last time before darting between the houses. It was nearly 3:00am. His father should be passed out by now. It was possible his dad didn't even know Trystan was gone. The room looked the same from the outside, so unless his dad opened the door, there was no way to know Trystan wasn't there.

Trystan didn't want to think about that right now. His heart was still enraptured by Mari. God, he loved her. Her scent was still on him. He inhaled deeply, basking in it. Mari's aroma made him lightheaded and giddy at the same time.

A smile snaked across Trystan's lips as he continued down the deserted streets alone. Porch lights flared on houses that were more expensive than anything he'd ever own. Glancing down the street, he caught the telltale silhouette of a cop car, and cut down a side street to avoid the police. A kid out alone, at 3:00am was looking for trouble. They'd haul him back home and all hell would break lose.

Trystan walked faster. Shoving his hands in his pockets he felt the phone Mari gave him. He didn't want to take it from her. It felt like a lavish gift that Trystan didn't deserve, but when he saw her face, he knew that she needed him to have it. It wasn't about stuff. It was about Mari. Trystan felt the edges of the little phone and wondered if he'd have to add minutes to it. He was totally broke, so unless it was prepaid for a while, that would create a problem. While Mari knew he didn't have a lot of money, no one realized how strapped Trystan was. He did everything he could to keep it hidden.

Arriving at the condo complex, Trystan walked past the group of older guys who were drunk. The night air was temperate so they were hanging out in front of their door, sitting on the front step like it was a patio. They tried to get Trystan to come over, but he'd rather die than get hooked on alcohol. That damn stuff was what caused of all his problems. It wasn't that his mom left them; it was that his dad refused to pick up the pieces and move on.

Trystan stopped at his front door and debated whether or not to go through his window. After a second, he chanced the door. Trystan slid his key in the lock and the door creaked open. Glancing around, Trystan didn't see his father, but he could hear his insanely loud snoring carrying from the back of the apartment.

"Thank God," Trystan sighed and locked the door behind him. That sound was music to his ears. It meant nothing could wake the old man, so Trystan headed for the shower. When he finished, Trystan unlocked the door to his room and closed it quietly, locking himself inside. Lowering himself to the floor, Trystan slept against the door to make sure his father didn't try anything.

The next morning Trystan awoke with the door slamming into his ribs. "Get up, Trystan." The door pulled back and slammed into him again. Trystan shook the sleep from his eyes and sat up and braced his back against the door to keep his dad out, but the old man didn't try to come in. He was just in a foul mood. "Go to school today, before they come looking for you. And I swear to God, if you ever do that again, I'll lock you in here and never come back."

Trystan's jaw tightened as his father spoke. If Trystan didn't have to come back, he wouldn't. There was nothing here for him. His life was ahead of him, but he couldn't leave. Not yet. Trystan swallowed his pride and said what his father was waiting to hear, "Yes, sir."

As soon as Trystan said those words, his father's footfalls headed away from his room. A few moments later the front door opened and closed. He was gone. Trystan sighed in relief. Sitting on the floor, he pulled his knees into his chest and wrapped his arms around them. Lowering his head to his knees, Trystan sat in the quiet wondering what he should do. If the army was out, then he had to find somewhere else to live, and fast.

—

Trystan sat in the cafeteria looking out the window for Mari. He had an apple in his hand and was about to take a bite when Seth sat down hard across from him. Trystan stopped and scowled. "I'm not in the mood, Seth."

Then, Seth did something very un-Seth-like and apologized. "He man, listen… I shouldn't have said that. I knew you wanted to hit that, but I thought she was just another chick."

Trystan rolled the apple in his palm, and lifted his gaze. He held his temper in check. Flatly, he replied, "I told you she wasn't, so don't try to bullshit me now."

Seth rolled his eyes, and slammed his hands on the table making the metal fittings underneath jingle. "I'm not bullshitting you. I'm sorry, okay? I said it. If she means that much to you, I won't go there again."

Trystan wanted to tell him about Mari, about how things changed, but he couldn't. He didn't know how Seth would react and he'd promised Mari he wouldn't. So Trystan nodded, "Fine. Enough of this crap. It's over."

Seth's face lit up. He reached across the table and slapped Trystan's shoulder just as Mari got out of her Mom's car outside. Seth's gaze followed Trystan's and landed on Mari. "You want me to help you get her?"

Trystan flinched. He turned back to Seth. "The answer to that would be, hell no. Don't even think about it. She's mine. I'll get her, eventually." Trystan's lips pulled into a grin. He already had her heart—she loved him. It made Trystan wish he could shout from the tabletops and dance across the hallways, but he didn't. Trystan was careful to leave his poker face in place.

"What is she? The only girl in the drama class that you haven't nailed?"

Trystan stood and glanced at the doors. "Something like that."

Tucker walked through, and turned his face at the two of them. It was as if he was looking for Trystan. Tucker waved Trystan over and Seth followed. "I need to speak with you, Scott. This weekend is the play and Brie refuses to go on with her nose the way it is. I told her we could cover it with stage make up, that no one would know, but she said she quit. Her parents pulled her out of the class. You have no co-star, Scott. Can you please go talk some sense into her? She listens to you."

Seth glanced at Trystan, but Trystan was still looking at Tucker. "Maybe, but I have a better idea." A sly smile lined Trystan's lips. He cut his gaze to the cafeteria doors just as Mari walked by and flicked his chin up. "Her."

Tucker's face pinched. "What? You can't be serious. Mari doesn't know all the—" Tucker stopped midsentence. His eyebrows shot up as a smile lifted the worry off his face. Looking back at Trystan, Tucker seemed amazed at the idea, "She knows all the lines."

"Yeah," Trystan nodded. "And she's been practicing with me longer than Brie. Mari can do it."

Tucker glanced at the hallway, and watched Mari walk away. "Fine. Talk to her. You both get A's for this. That might not matter to you, but it does for her. She's the one that caused this issue in the first place by punching Brie in the face."

Seth laughed and jumped from one foot to the other like a happy monkey. He pressed his palms together, "No way! Girl fight and I missed it? Little goodie-two-shoes took a swing at the slut?"

Tucker opened his mouth to say something and then snapped it shut again. He shook his head and walked away.

Seth turned to Trystan, "Seriously? Your new conquest bitch-slapped your old girlfriend? Ha! I didn't think Mari had it in her." Suddenly Seth seemed more interested in Mari, which wasn't good.

"Brie had it coming," Trystan snapped. "And now she thinks she can screw everyone else by not showing up on Friday." Trystan grinned, thinking about acting opposite Mari, and that kiss at the end of act 2. Oh God, he'd get to kiss Mari like that in front of everyone without anyone thinking anything was going on with them. "This is going to be awesome."

CHAPTER 12

~MARI~

"I'm not an actor, Trystan. I can't do what you do." He asked me to take Brie's role. Part of me wanted to, but the other part said there was no way I could pull it off.

Trystan sat on the table in front of me. We were in the prop room under the stage. He waited to tell me until we had some time alone. Trystan's hands found my shoulders and he gripped them gently. "Yes, you can. You already have, and you did it a lot better than Brie."

My mind raced. If I said yes, this would be the third time I'd pissed off Brie in a really short amount of time. It just wasn't smart. "Trystan, I wouldn't know where to stand or how to respond to the other actors. This isn't my thing. I'd suck it up."

"Tucker said you have a C in his class right now. He wanted me to tell you that you'll get an automatic A if you take her spot." He watched my face as he spoke the magic words.

My face pinched. I wanted to say no, but that was too tempting. "Damn him—Tucker, I mean. That C will cause as much trouble as Brie." I started thinking out loud without realizing it.

"What?" Trystan asked, confused.

"The C. My dad is a psycho with grades. I'll catch hell for it. But, if I take Brie's place so I get the A, I'm going to catch hell from her. I'm already on her shit list." I sighed and looked into Trystan's face. "It's not much of a choice."

"I can take care of Brie."

"Brie's suing me, well, my Dad—" I just blurted it out. I'd managed to leave out that part last night. The conversation skirted around it. I made it sound like a teacher tattled on me and not Brie's father. Trystan's hands slipped off my shoulders, as his jaw dropped open. “because I punched her. That’s what caused the fight the other night with my Dad. It was Brie.”

Trystan pressed his eyes closed and shook his head, like he couldn’t believe it. He stood and paced, thinking. The muscles in his jaw worked as he walked. Trystan crossed his arms over his chest. The dark blue tee shirt he wore showed off his sapphire eyes. I couldn’t help but stare at him. He was beautiful.

When Trystan stopped, he said, “Brie is a pain in the ass, but we have a shot at handling her. Your father, on the other hand, we have no control over him at all. I’d get the grade and deal with the Brie, if I were you."

I smiled at him. That was what I was thinking, I just wished there was another option. Standing, I walked over to him, "And this decision has nothing to do with the kiss at the end of the second act?"

"Do you know how hard it is to stand in front of you and not touch you? Right now—" he shook his head, "I can't even tell you what I want to do right now. It's more than a kiss Mari. It's more time together, more kissing, and more you. Of course I want you to say yes." Trystan looked down into my eyes. He held my gaze making butterflies erupt in my stomach.

"Yes." My voice was light.

Trystan blinked at me, like he hadn't heard me right. "Seriously?"

I nodded and stepped closer to him, slipping my arms around his waist. "Yes. You're right. I know the part and I really don't mind kissing you, actually I look forward to it." I ran my fingers through his hair while I looked into his eyes. Trystan's gaze remained locked on mine.

"You're wicked, you know that? The only thing I can think about now is kissing you." Trystan's fingers pulled at my waist until my chest was firmly against his. The way we fit together made me feel tingles all over. It felt like I was blasted with a heater when he touched me. Suddenly I was hot and breathing like I'd run miles. He didn't even kiss me yet. We were just talking about it.

"All part of my plan, kiss assassin." I flirted back.

"I wonder if tha—" Trystan didn't get to finish his remark because I reached up and grabbed his neck, and pulled his lips down on mine. Trystan's hands held me tight as he kissed me back, his lips gently tasting mine before he lost all control and kissed me harder. I think I forgot to breathe at one point. The whole thing was perfect; the way he held me, the way he kissed me, the way he said my name like there was no one else and there never would be.

When we pulled apart, I sucked in ragged breaths and tried to calm down. Trystan smiled at me. I grinned back, and swatted his arm. "I'm wicked? That was supposed to be a little kiss?"

"I didn't see you keeping it little," he said, bouncing slightly on the balls of his feet. Trystan was happy, happy like I'd never seen him before. Every inch of Trystan was alive and resonating with mirth.

"Ha! Like that's my fault. It's kind of hard to do things half way with you. When you kissed me, while we were rehearsing, I almost died. No one's ever kissed me the way you do." I sat down hard on the couch, fanning myself. My heart was still pounding in my ears.

Trystan jumped onto the couch beside me. "And who else kissed you?"

My spine straightened and I turned slowly to look at him. I didn't want to talk about that. Instead of answering, a blush stained my cheeks. Trystan took my hands, his eyes glittering with curiosity, and said, "Or should I ask how many? Are you really a sexual deviant? Could I be that lucky?"

I laughed. I couldn't help it. "A sexual deviant?"

"Back on track, Mari, my love. How many others have there been?"

When I hesitated, he said, "I'll tell you mine if you tell me yours."

"I don't want to know how many girls you've slept with! God, Trystan." I pulled my hands away and rubbed my eyes.

He was still smiling, "Are you sure? You might be surprised. I'm not the male slut everyone thinks I am. I'm only a little slutty." He pinched his fingers together, leaving a tiny space between.

That got my attention. "What do you mean?"

Trystan shook his head, still smiling, not offering more information. "You tell me your's first."

"You're evil," I laughed. Trystan waggled his eyebrows at me and grinned widely. "Fine…I had one serious boyfriend. We didn't do everything, but it didn't matter. He still crushed me when we broke up. He goes to another school, so at least I don't have to see him every day." Trystan kept his hand on mine, rubbing the back of my palm. I glanced up at him from under my lashes, feeling foolish. "I haven't been with anyone. Seth's nickname for me is accurate."

Trystan leaned forward and kissed me on the end of my nose. Grinning, he sat back slowly. "You're perfect, Mari. Holding out for the right guy isn't stupid, and guys who say it is just want to get in your pants."

"Like you?" I said, kiddingly.

"Like me," Trystan continued to hold my hand, his fingers gently brushing against the side of my fingers as he gazed at me. "Well, like me before I met you, and I've heard your chastity sermons for a few years now. Let's just say you weaseled your way into my brain and I didn't hook up with every girl I came across. The rumors of my conquests have been greatly exaggerated." Trystan lifted my hand to his lips and kissed it.

"Meaning?" My heart was racing. Was he saying what I thought he was saying? That couldn't be true, but I could tell from the expression in his eyes that it was—this was a secret that he was happy to share—one that he couldn't wait to tell me.

"Meaning, I'm still a novice at this. I only had one relationship and it was with Brie." He cringed. "Obviously I'm a total moron and have no idea what I'm doing. Besides her, I messed around and made-out, but…" Trystan looked at me for a second and then looked to the side, his lips curling into a bashful smile. "Are you really going to make me say it?"

I blinked at him, assuming I was dumb as a post and not following. "I think I have to. Are you seriously telling me that you were only with one girl? What about all that stuff Seth said?"

"Seth's a moron. He's all bluster, Mari. Have you ever seen him do anything but suck face with a girl?"

I cringed, "No."

"Well, same thing for me. Appearances are deceiving. I hope you won't use this information to tarnish my bad-boy persona at school. I like all the ladies drooling when I walk by." He was laughing now, watching me with laughter in his eyes.

Grinning, I swatted him with my hand, "Oh, gross! Now you sound like him!"

Trystan and I laughed and kissed until the bell rang. When I emerged from the auditorium, I ran into Katie.

She instantly noticed my swollen lips and blotchy skin. "Sucking face? With whom might this suckage be occurring? Or should I go look for him?" She glanced behind me, hoping to see the object of my affection.

I yanked her arm and led her down the hall. "No one."

"Yeah, right. And that's why we're running away, so I can't see the invisible man who ate your strawberry lip gloss." Katie's tone was light, teasing. She kept looking over her shoulder like the guy would magically appear.

"Where's Mathboy when I need him?" I glanced around hoping he was nearby.

"He's my sexy nerd, and he's not going to save you from the slew of questions I'm going to hurl at your head." We walked into the classroom and Katie set her books on her desk.

I looked back to the spot where Brie sat. Her chair was empty. I swallowed hard wondering if I could really go up against her and walk away intact.

CHAPTER 13

~TRYSTAN~

Rehearsal was much more enjoyable with Mari in his arms and Brie god-knows-where. Trystan tried as hard as he could to live in the now, but he couldn't shake the feeling that it would all slip between his fingers at any moment. The more time he spent with Mari, the more they kissed, the more he realized he wanted her—and not in a temporary kind of way. There was something about Mari that made him come alive when she was around.

All the years of jaded cynicism melted into giddy glee around her.

Tucker barely corrected Mari. She remembered everything, because she'd been prompting the entire time. She'd only lost a couple of days when Tucker threw her out. The cast had a different feel with Mari among them. She affected Trystan's performance for the better and everyone around him strove to be as charismatic as Trystan. It was a domino effect and it started with Mari.

When Tucker first announced Brie's replacement, no one though Mari could do it. She sat in the shadows, reading books—she wasn't an actor—but Mari proved them wrong by the end of the first scene.

Tucker didn't stop the play, he let the entire thing run from start to end and when they finished, Tucker just sat there, staring at them with one eyebrow lifted too high.

The entire cast stood on stage, waiting for him to say something.

"Did he have a stroke?" Tia whispered out of the side of her mouth to the girl standing next to her.

Tucker laughed one sharp, "HA!" And then stood in his seat, clapping his beefy hands until they were all deaf. "I couldn't have imagined that a high school cast was capable of this skill level. Trystan and Mari, I don't know what it is, but there's something about you two that pulled the whole performance up a few notches. I didn't think this was possible." Tucker stood there, arms folded across his chest, shaking his head.

Trystan spoke to Tia out of the side of his mouth, "We must have really sucked before." All the girls instantly fell into a fit of giggles. Trystan waggled his eyebrows at Mari, who grinned at him in return.

Everyone looked around, wondering if they could take a break, or if they needed to do another run through. Tucker finally realized this and said, "We're done. It can't get better than this!" Murmuring to himself, Tucker turned and grabbed his folders and jacket.

The lights were turned off as Tucker made his way to the door.

The stage lights remained on for another moment while the kid in the lighting cage got his books. Everyone ran from the room like rats from a sinking ship, except Mari who hung back in the wing, waiting for Trystan.

"You ready?" he asked.

She nodded. "Yeah."

They walked out of the school farther apart than either of them wanted to be. Mari looked over her shoulder and smiled at Trystan. Her dark curls blew like ribbons in the wind. Trystan and Mari already discussed walking places together. They decided that they'd act the way they usually did. He walked her to her block sometimes, before crossing the railroad tracks and heading towards his house. Mari knew he lived in the condos in the rough part of town, but she'd never been there.

"That went well." Trystan smirked at her. Mari smiled back, her dark eyes caressing his face as soft as a touch. His stomach dropped. God, he wanted to kiss her.

"I was surprised it went that well."

"I wasn't. I knew you'd rock it. I mean, you have a natural talent for this kind of stuff. You always have." Trystan stood at the street corner waiting for the light to change, when he felt Mari's eyes on the side of his face. "What?"

She shook her head, "Nothing, it's just every time I think I know you, something else comes out."

"I *adore* you. You know that."

"It's not that. It's your conviction. You said that with total certainty, like you knew I could do it when I didn't even know that. How can you talk like that?"

"How can I not? Did you see you up there? It was amazing. Why haven't you tried out for a part before?"

Mari shrugged, "Daddy doesn't think it's a productive use of my time."

"I know he thinks he's helping you, but he's holding you back." Trystan looked at her as they crossed the street. "You have so much potential and he's channeling it into this little tunnel that sucks the light out of you."

Mari's gaze was on the ground in front of her. "There are some things that can't be changed—like parents—I'm stuck with mine." She glanced up at him.

Trystan knew what she meant. It pierced him at his core. "No, you can't pick your parents, but you get to choose what life you live. Mari, I don't know what's going to happen, but I want you to know this… you're capable of so much more." They'd stopped walking and were standing face to face in front of Mari's house. Trystan wanted to touch her face and pull her in and feel her lips against his.

"So are you, Day Jones," she said, knocking him off kilter. "What's holding you back?" Those brown eyes searched his face.

Trystan tensed. "That's different."

"Is it? 'Cause it looks kind of the same. You get a choice. You're beyond exceptional. You're pure magic, Trystan, and yet, you hide it from everyone. No one really knows who you are. For some reason you let me see, and I can't look away. I can't understand why you'd leave your musical talent hidden. It's a solid future, enough money for college, and a solid way to get your life started, but you won't take it. Why won't you take it? What are you afraid of?" Mari said these things looking into his eyes. She spoke softly, like she was afraid he'd run.

Trystan's heart beat harder and harder as she spoke. Every truth she struck rang out with pristine clarity. She saw him clearly, which was both amazing and terrifying at the same time. He felt his hands shake and slipped them in his pockets. He wanted to tell her. He wanted to say that it was his father, that he'd been beaten and neglected his entire life, but he couldn't. Trystan's sardonic smile laced across his lips.

Mari's gaze narrowed in response. "Don't say something witty right now. You're asking me to do the same thing, to tell them that the life they picked out for me isn't the one I want, but you won't do it yourself. You're not a hypocrite, Trystan, so there's got to be another reason for it, one you won't tell me—one I can't figure out on my own."

Before Trystan had a chance to respond, Mari's front door opened and a man stood there. He was tall and thin with waves of dark hair slicked back neatly. He had on dress slacks the color of caramel and a dark silk sweater that did nothing to block out the cold. The man was covered in subtle status symbols. From the way he looked at them, Trystan knew this was Mari's father.

"Mari! Get in here!" His tone was clipped. Trystan watched him go back into the house, instantly disliking him. He snapped at Mari like she was a dog.

Mari looked over her shoulder when she was called, then said to Trystan, "I have to go. Come later, okay? After 7:00pm."

"I wouldn't miss it."

—

Trystan avoided his home at all cost, but he needed a shower and clean clothes. When Trystan arrived, his dad wasn't home. *Thank God.* It was still too early, but you never knew with him. Some days dad would show up early and Trystan didn't know why. The way Trystan figured it, he had just enough time to take a shower and get out.

Trystan washed quickly, happy to get clean before seeing Mari again. He pulled on the same pair of jeans he wore earlier, but he had no shirt. Rummaging through his dad's closet, Trystan pulled out a tee shirt and put it on. Trystan combed his damp hair, pushing it out of his eyes. Thoughts about Mari and what she said kept drifting through his head. When Mari spoke like that it was contagious. She believed he could make it as Day Jones. Her confidence made Trystan feel like he could do anything, be anything, that there were no limits.

The Day Jones phenomenon was still raging and getting more insane by the day. Rabid fans wanted more. They wouldn't let it die, and since Trystan's computer was gone, he didn't know what level of insanity things had grown to. Last he looked, the number of comments had more than tripled. Agents and record labels were begging him to contact them. There was no way Trystan could read the comments all in one sitting. It would take days.

Maybe Mari was right. Maybe confessing that he was Day Jones was the best option, the best way out of this hell hole. Trystan liked the idea of performing, of singing on a stage, and of everything that goes with being in the limelight—except the paparazzi. They'd dig into his past and find out everything. It was too much to even think about. Mari was right. There was something holding him back, something that prevented him from ever coming forward as Day Jones. His father.

As if he conjured the old man from thin air, Trystan heard the front door slam shut. Trystan swore and ducked into his room quickly. His dad wasn't supposed to be home for another hour, at least.

His father's garbled words rang out. "I busted my ass with the company for twenty years!" There was a loud crash, the sound of something heavy hitting the wall. "And how do they thank me for it?"

Another crash, followed by the sound of shattering glass.

Trystan's eyes grew wide. He knew he had to get out now, but his father was blocking the exit. Trystan turned toward the window, wondering if the bars falling to the ground would make too much noise. Looking back at the door, Trystan decided that it was too risky. Besides, his father would know that he'd left his room if the rusted bars were on the ground. Like it or not, Trystan was stuck here for a few more weeks. He had to make it through. The sounds of things being destroyed suddenly stopped. The apartment was silent. The hairs on the back of Trystan's neck stood on end as a shadow stretched across the floor. His father stepped into the doorway, irate. His muscles were corded tight, ready to explode.

Glaring at Trystan, his dad growled, "You little shit, you're home? You hear me yelling and screaming and you didn't bother to come see what was wrong?" His father's bloodshot eyes locked on his. Dad was still wearing his dress shirt, but the tie and jacket were gone. It was unlike him to get plastered before heading home. That kind of awesomeness was reserved for Trystan alone.

Trystan didn't answer. There was nothing he could say that would make this better. His father's gaze swept over his son's damp hair and clean T-shirt. Recognition formed on Dad's face. "Who said you could take my shirt?"

Trystan knew his silence was being taken as defiance. Everything in his body told Trystan to run, but he was trapped in his hell-hole of a room with his dad barring the exit. "All my clothes seem to have been thrown out."

"So you steal my stuff? That's your solution to everything, isn't it? You see what you want and take it. There's no talking to you. Even now, with the way you look at me like your better." As his dad spoke, he walked into the room. With every step his dad took forward, Trystan took a step back.

Fuck. He was going to get trapped in the corner. Trystan had to get out of there. Every muscle in his body tensed, waiting for the old man's fists to start flying. Trystan had not seen his dad this irate before, not during daylight hours anyway. "I'm not better than anyone," Trystan breathed the words through his teeth, his chest tightening as he spoke.

"You're a goddamn lair and a thief."

Trystan stepped away again. "What happened today? Why are you even here?"

His father's face pulled into a grim smile. "That fucking company that I spent my entire life working for let me go. They merged with another office and decided to downsize. Did they bother to tell any of us that? No. We walked in today and guess what? Surprise! After working my ass off for two decades, I have no job." He ranted, anger surging through him as he spoke. His gaze narrowed on his son. "And then, I come home and find my kid stealing my stuff. What the fuck gives you the right?" He was yelling now, his hands flying through the air.

Trystan's back was nearly against the wall. He'd rather fly into his dad's fists than get trapped in the corner. *Don't fight back*, he chanted in his mind, over and over again. *Get around him and run.* But Trystan couldn't see how.

Swallowing hard, Trystan said, "No one gave me the right." Trystan grabbed the shirt and pulled it over his head as fast as he could and threw it at his dad. The shirt hit his father in chest and fell to the floor.

The anger in his father's face exploded. Dad's normally nice features contorted with rage. He lunged at Trystan, his hands open like he planned on strangling him.

Trystan dogged to the side at the last second and darted past his dad into the hallway. Quickly, he reached for the door and pulled it shut. His dad started screaming profanity at him. It was the worst verbal assault he'd ever had. It combined every failure, every short coming, and every fear that lurked inside Trystan's mind. Trystan tried to let the words slip past him, but every single one lodged into his skin like darts. By the time his dad tried pulling on the door, Trystan had the knob in his and was twisting the lock. When Trystan heard the metallic scrape, he knew the door was locked.

Resting, Trystan pressed his head to the door for a second, thankful that he made it away without getting hit, when something slammed into it and shook the frame. The plaster on the ceiling cracked and sprinkled on his bare shoulders like baby powder. Looking up, he saw thin lines spidering away from the doorframe.

Trystan stepped back before the second blow came. That shot was harder and shook the wall. A picture frame crashed to the floor and shattered. His father was cracking the doorframe. Trystan turned to run. He thought he was safe for a second, but he wasn't. From the look of it, Trystan only had one more hit to get himself out of harm's way. That door was coming down.

Trystan ran for the front of the apartment, cutting down the narrow hall as fast as he could. A loud cracking noise came from behind, as Trystan reached for the front doorknob. His father bellowed and fell through the rubble. He stumbled to his feet fast for a drunk guy. The expression on Dad's face was beyond livid, more like psychotically angry. Trystan never pushed his dad that far before. He never fought back, he never intended to. Locking the door didn't count, but the expression on his father's face said otherwise.

Fear snaked through Trystan, strangling him. This was something he couldn't undo. What happened tonight couldn't be changed. Trystan didn't mean for it to happen. He wished he never came home. Before Trystan could think another thought, his dad came barreling down the hall like a rabid bear, practically foaming at the mouth, with a thirst for blood in his eyes. Part of him wanted this to be a nightmare, to believe that his father wouldn't hurt him, but he'd been alive too long to think that.

Trystan yanked the door open, intending to run through and escape into the cold night air, but when he jerked the door open someone was there.

"Mari?" he gasped, taken by surprise.

Mari stood there with a red nose and eyes like she'd been crying. Huffing like she'd run to him, she looked past him and then back at his eyes, "Trystan, what's wrong?" The look on Trystan's face said everything was wrong. He couldn't believe she was at the door. Now.

"Run, Mari. Go. Don't come back." Trystan turned away from her just as his dad barreled into him. Their bodies collided smashing the door shut before Mari could blink. A bloodcurdling scream erupted from her throat, shattering the still night.

THE SECRET LIFE OF TRYSTAN SCOTT
Vol. 4

Coming Winter 2013

Make sure you don't miss it!

MORE BOOKS BY H.M. WARD

DEMON KISSED

CURSED

TORN

SATAN'S STONE

THE 13th PROPHECY

ASSASSIN: FALL OF THE GOLDEN VALEFAR

VALEFAR VOL. 1 & 2

STONE PRISON

BANE

CATALYST

SECRETS SERIES

SCANDALOUS

LOVE THIS BOOK?

Share the love and leave a review! I'll be your best friend forever and ever. ;)

Visit this author at:

www.YAParanormalRomance.com

www.facebook.com/VampireApocalypse

www.twitter.com/hmward

Made in the USA
Lexington, KY
07 October 2013